P9-CDM-029

W

Conley, Robert J
The dark way

DATE DUE			
MAY 1 1993			
JUL 2 1993			
AUG 6 1993			
DEC 1 1993			

MYNDERSE LIBRARY

Seneca Falls, N.Y.

The Real People
Book Two

THE DARK WAY

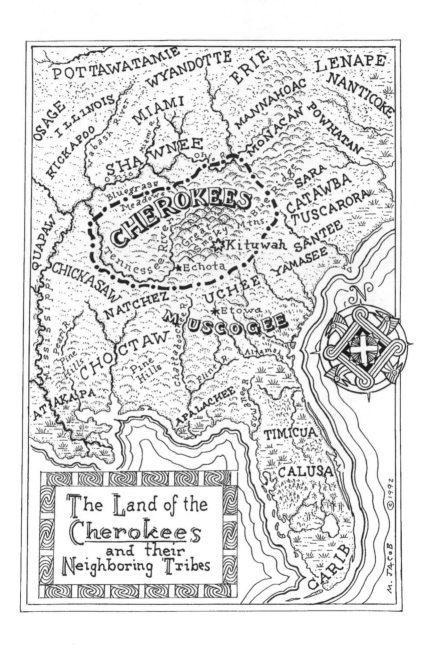

The Land of the Cherokees and their Neighboring Tribes

ROBERT J. CONLEY

The Dark Way

A Double D Western
DOUBLEDAY
New York   London   Toronto   Sydney   Auckland

A Double D Western
PUBLISHED BY DOUBLEDAY
a division of Bantam Doubleday Dell Publishing Group, Inc.
666 Fifth Avenue, New York, New York 10103

DOUBLE D WESTERN, DOUBLEDAY,
and the portrayal of the letters DD
are trademarks of Doubleday, a division of
Bantam Doubleday Dell Publishing Group, Inc.

Map and illustrations by Murv Jacob

Library of Congress Cataloging-in-Publication Data

Conley, Robert J.
The dark way/Robert J. Conley.—1st ed.
 p. cm.—(The Real people; bk. 2) (A Double D western)
1. Cherokee Indians—Fiction. I. Title. II. Series:
Conley, Robert J. Real people; bk. 2.
PS3553.O494D37 1993
813'.54—dc20 92-24812
CIP

ISBN 0-385-41933-3
March 1993
First Edition

10 9 8 7 6 5 4 3 2 1

THE DARK WAY

One

TWO DEER and six turkeys. No one else had been asked to supply so much. Asked? No. He had been told, ordered by the effeminate priest to go out and kill two deer and six turkeys and bring them back for the coming big ceremony. At one point, briefly, he had tried to tell himself that his assignment was a reflection of his reputation as a hunter, that the *Kutani* knew that Edohi could easily provide more meat than any other two men. But he knew better than that. And if he hadn't known, the arrogance of Two Heads had been enough to tell him the truth. Two Heads the priest. The *Kutani*. Edohi's lips twisted involuntarily into an ugly snarl at the thought of what his childhood companion had become.

An apprentice *Kutani* had come to Edohi's town of Ijodi. It had been easy to tell that the young man had run all the way from Men's Town. He was out of breath and had delivered his message in short puffs. He had found

Edohi at the *gatayusti* playing field near the townhouse. No one had been playing. Edohi had been lounging there with his uncle, Hemp Carrier, and other men of his clan, *Ani-Tsisqua*, the Bird People. The *Kutani*, not much more than a boy, had come running up to them, puffing and gasping, and he had asked for Edohi.

"I am he," said Edohi. "What do you want with me?"

"You are ordered to go to Men's Town," the young priest said. "The *Kutani* Two Heads wants to speak to you."

Edohi had just looked at the young man, had not responded.

"You can return with me," said the priestling.

"I suppose," said Edohi, "that you will run all the way back again."

Hemp Carrier and the others laughed. The young man blushed and opened his mouth as if to respond, but Edohi saved him the trouble and the further embarrassment.

"Go along," he said. "I'll be there. I'll go over to Men's Town."

Then he had waited a while, still talking with his kinsmen. The young man had indeed left Ijodi running back toward Men's Town.

"What do you suppose that's all about?" said Beavertail, a clan brother to Edohi.

"I don't know," Edohi said with a shrug. "I'll find out in a while, I guess."

"I'll bet it has something to do with the big ceremony the priests are planning," said Hemp Carrier.

And Hemp Carrier had been right. Edohi had waited for a while, out of spite, and then he had walked at a leisurely pace over to Men's Town. There on the parapet walk behind the wall stood the same young priest, Two Heads's messenger boy, apparently awaiting Edohi's arrival.

"Wait there, Edohi," he shouted, and he disappeared beneath the wall. And Edohi had waited. It had been a long wait. Two Heads was obviously getting even with him for his having responded to the *Kutani*'s command so slowly. Edohi had just about decided to leave when Two Heads at last made his appearance. The pompous priest did not come outside the walls to talk with Edohi. Instead he appeared above in the same spot the apprentice had been so that he could look over the wall and down on Edohi and issue decrees. Edohi seethed inside but kept quiet.

"Edohi," said Two Heads, a mocking edge to his voice, "you are to bring two deer and six turkeys to Men's Town in seven days for the ceremony for the rain. Two deer and six turkeys. In seven days."

Edohi's flesh felt hot with rage, but he contained it. He wanted to rush through the gateway into the forbidden town, climb the ladder to the parapet walk and hurl Two Heads headlong over the wall.

"Do you hear me?" said Two Heads.

"I hear you, priest," said Edohi, and he turned to leave. That had been five days ago. Edohi had returned to Ijodi and told his clansmen about his assignment from Men's Town. Then he had gone to his wife's house to tell her.

"When will you go?" asked Corn Flower.

"In the morning, I guess," he had answered. "I guess I'll go."

"You have to go," she said. "Don't you? When the *Ani-Kutani* tell someone to do something, that person has no choice."

"I don't think that's right," he said.

"Perhaps not, but it is so."

Edohi had not wanted to leave Corn Flower, but he had left Ijodi the next morning anyway. He was still fuming inside over the arrogance of Two Heads and the unjust power the *Ani-Kutani* exercised over all of the Real People. He decided that it would probably be best for him to get out into the woods and away from people for a few days alone, to hunt and to cool off, to try to get his mind on something besides the priests.

It had not worked, not right away. Edohi thought constantly of the priests. It was true, he knew, that the *Ani-Kutani* interceded with all the spirits on behalf of the Real People, that their rites and ceremonies kept the Real People walking in precarious balance on the middle world. At least that was their claim, and until recently, no one had questioned the assertion. But lately people had begun to express doubts about the claims, the authority, the behavior and the motives of the priests. Edohi was not alone in that. One of the most outspoken critics of the *Ani-Kutani* was his mother's brother, Hemp Carrier. And at least in private, it seemed, just about everyone was willing to voice complaints.

Yet nothing changed, and Edohi could see no way in which things could change. Could someone talk sense into Standing-in-the-Doorway? No one would dare try. The head *Kutani* seemed to strike fear into the hearts of all the people with just a look. And there was no one else with the power to alter the behavior of the priests. Standing-in-the-Doorway was all-powerful. He was the only one. Edohi recalled the first time he himself had encountered Standing-in-the-Doorway, the time when he and Corn Flower and Two Heads, then Acorn, had been childhood companions and had been stalking the *Kutani*'s trail only to be caught in their own trap. The priest had somehow known what they were doing and had waited for them on the trail. Edohi could remember the cold fear that had coursed through his body at the sudden appearance of the priest there in the path before them. No, he thought. No one would dare to voice their complaints to Standing-in-the-Doorway.

So Edohi hunted. Two deer and six turkeys. Had Standing-in-the-Doorway, he wondered, initiated that command, or had Two Heads just taken it upon himself to lord it over his former companion? He didn't know. He could not know. So he hunted for two deer and six turkeys. But he realized that his mind was not really on the hunt. He was not actually hunting. He was wandering aimlessly in the woods. What would happen, he asked himself, if he returned with only one deer and six turkeys, or two deer and five turkeys? What would happen if he failed to return with any game? Would the ceremony be canceled, or would it take place? Would it fail? Would the people gathered there starve for want of two deer and six turkeys? Would Edohi himself be summarily executed for having refused to obey an order from the *Kutani?* He didn't know. He had never before actually been ordered to do anything by anybody.

But there was the ceremony. He tried to remind himself that his disdain for Two Heads was trivial compared to the importance of the ceremony. It had been a long time without rain, and the land all around was suffering. The crops of the Real People were poor, and even the river was getting low. Edohi could not remember a time when it had not rained for such a long while. That was another reason the people were losing faith in the *Ani-Kutani*. It was the job of the priests to ensure adequate rain. Everyone knew that Standing-in-the-Doorway had sent three priests to the west to search for the house of Thunder and to bring back the rain. It had been a long time, and the three priests had not returned. No one knew how far they would have to travel in order to fulfill their mission, or how long such a trip would take. Even so, most people seemed to have given up on them. They are hopelessly lost, people were saying, or, they are dead. They have encountered some warlike people who have killed them. Some even believed that the priests might have arrived at the western edge of the world only to be crushed to death by the Sky Vault while they were trying to sneak under to the other side. One old man speculated that they had made it to the other side and found their way to the Darkening Land. Now, he said, they cannot find their way back. "No one has ever come back from the Darkening Land." Edohi had no idea what had become of the priests, but, like almost everyone else, he had given up on either their return or their success.

Even Standing-in-the-Doorway, it seemed, had given up on them. Otherwise he would not have announced the ceremony. It was to be the biggest ceremony anyone had ever seen. Even the old people were saying that there had not been one like it in their lifetimes. It was an ancient ceremony, reserved for times of great catastrophe, and Standing-in-the-Doorway was going to revive it because of the drought. Where all else had failed, it would succeed. It would bring the rain. No one knew the details of the ancient ceremony, but word had seeped out from Men's Town that it would include at least one major surprise, one ancient practice long since abandoned. It would be a ceremony of desperation for a desperate time.

People would gather around Men's Town from all of the towns of the Real People. Uncle Hemp Carrier had said that Standing-in-the-Doorway's real reason for the ceremony was to stop the people from grumbling and complaining, to divert their thoughts for a while and hope that the rains would come.

"But no one complains to Standing-in-the-Doorway," Edohi had said, "and if no one tells him, then how does he know?"

"He knows," said Hemp Carrier. "We can be sure of that."

So now Edohi was hunting. Two deer and six turkeys.

Back at Ijodi the women were busy, too. They were preparing food for the big ceremony at Men's Town. There would be lots of people there to be fed. Of course, they would all bring food, but Ijodi was close to Men's Town, and Ijodi would shoulder the heaviest load. Some of the women were in the woods or along the riverbank gathering what wild foods could be found. The gardens, private and communal, had already been mostly harvested. But all of the crops were poor for lack of water. The Spoiler was pounding hickory nuts in her *kanona*, her beater, and she was grumbling as her daughter Corn Flower approached with a basket in her arms.

"They are too dry," said the Spoiler. "The *kanutche* will not be good."

"I've brought some more," said Corn Flower.

"They'll be as dry as these," said the Spoiler.

Corn Flower put the basket on the ground there beside the *kanona* stump.

"Where is the Outcast?" she asked.

"I sent my Shawnee slave to the garden with your sister," said the Spoiler. "I sent them to gather what we left before because we thought it wasn't good enough. Now it seems that we'll have to use everything."

"But what if he tries to run away or—?"

"Don't worry," said the Spoiler. "There are men out there watching. Your sister will be all right, and my Shawnee dog will not escape."

"You've kept him for a while now," said Corn Flower. "Have you decided not to kill him?"

The expression on the Spoiler's face hardened even more.

"I haven't decided yet what I'll do with him," she said, and she pounded harder and faster with her long beater pole.

"Let me do that for a while, Mother," said Corn Flower, reaching for the pole. The Spoiler let her take it, bent to pick up the basket from the ground and poured some of its contents into the hollow of the *kanona* stump.

"I don't know what those priests think they're doing," she said. "It's taking all of our stored foods to prepare for this ceremony, and at a time when the stores will not be easily replenished—if at all. They're going to ruin us."

"It's to bring the rain," said Corn Flower.

"Yes," said the Spoiler. "And that's why they sent those three to the west, too. That hasn't worked, has it? Why should we think that this will work?"

Corn Flower pounded the hickory nuts with rhythmic strokes.

"I don't know, Mother," she said. "I don't know."

Across the way, peering around the far corner of another house, bedecked in his priestly robes, a surly pout on his smooth face, Two Heads lurked, and he watched.

Like-a-Pumpkin had traveled as fast as he could all day long. He kept looking back over his shoulder expecting to see some of the vile, fierce men coming after him, but he did not see them. At some point along the way, he had realized that he was going east. He was headed for home, and that realization had caused him a moment of panic. He did not recall having made that decision. It had not yet rained. He had not yet seen any rain clouds in the sky. He had not accomplished his sacred mission. One of his companions was dead. The other was a captive somewhere in the filthy camp he had left behind him. His writing implements were lost, along with his precious sheaf of bark pages, and it had not rained. He was headed for home, and he had failed. The imposing figure of Standing-in-the-Doorway rose before him in his mind, yet he did not turn back. He was afraid. He could not go on alone into the unknown West searching for the house of Thunder, a house that might not even exist. He kept walking, moving east.

Edohi sat beneath a large oak tree. Everything around him was dry and dusty. Even the hot air was dry and dusty to his mouth and throat and lungs. He had been in the forest for four days. Twice he had come upon turkeys, and he could easily have killed more than the six he had been commanded to furnish. He had not killed one. I'll see more, he had told himself. And earlier in the day, he had watched four deer browsing at the edge of a clearing. Them, too, he had watched and left alone. They had gone their way, and he had gone his. It will be better, he had told himself, to wait and make my kills on the sixth day or the seventh and then head right back with them while they're still fresh. So why, he asked himself, had he left Ijodi so early? To be sure he would find plenty of game? No. That was not it. He had known he would find it. Besides, what good was it to locate the game early if he did not kill it when he saw it?

He admitted to himself then that he had left early because he had wanted to get away from everyone, even, he acknowledged with some feeling of guilt, from Corn Flower. He had been angry, almost furious, and he had been afraid of what he might say or do. He had felt a need to get away and be alone and calm himself, and it had worked. After four days in the forest, he was calm. He was able to think about the *Ani-Kutani*, even specifically about Two Heads, without clenching his teeth or his fists, without feeling his face flush in anger, without trembling with rage.

He leaned back against the scratchy, dry, brittle bark of the big oak and listened to the sounds of the forest. A mild breeze rattled the dry leaves overhead. A squirrel somewhere near scolded loudly, probably annoyed at Edohi's rude intrusion into its territory. And from somewhere a little farther off, a blue jay was doing its best to imitate the cry of a sparrow hawk. He didn't fool Edohi. Then from off in the distance a turkey sounded its bellicose tremolo. Did Edohi want to find it and kill it? No. He did not.

He wondered again what would happen if he simply failed to show up with his contribution to the celebration. There were lots of reasons, he thought, a man might not return from the forest on the day he had planned to return. He might have an accident and break an arm or a leg. He might come across enemies out on a raid and have to fight, be injured or captured or both. Or—he thought of the *Nunnehi*, the Immortals, that strange race of people who looked and spoke just like the Real People, but who were, most of the time, invisible. The Real People believed that the Immortals had towns all around, but the towns, like their inhabitants, were usually invisible. Sometimes, it was said, their drumming and singing could be heard coming from the invisible towns. Edohi had never heard it, but he didn't doubt the word of those who claimed that they had. It was also said that in the past when some of the Real People were in danger of being overwhelmed by a large enemy force, Immortals had suddenly appeared in large enough numbers to rout the enemy.

But Edohi was thinking about their effect upon one's

perception of time. He thought about the old story of the man who had gone out alone to construct a fish trap in the river. It was about midday, and he had gone out early in the morning. Another man, someone he had never seen before, appeared just behind him. The sudden appearance startled the fisherman, but the man appeared to be friendly enough, so he relaxed.

"You've been working here a long time," said the stranger. "It's time to eat. I live near here. Come home with me, and I'll give you something to eat."

The fisherman accepted the stranger's hospitality, but he was puzzled when he had followed the man home. He was almost sure that he had walked by this place earlier in the day, but there had not been a house there. He went in anyway and shared a good meal with the man and his family. Later he thanked them and headed for home. He had not walked far when he looked back over his shoulder, and he was startled once more. The house was not there. He walked on, and soon he saw some of his friends and relatives up ahead coming toward him. As soon as they recognized him, they rushed to meet him.

"We were worried about you," they said. "We were afraid that you'd been killed."

"Why?" he asked. "What are you talking about?"

"You've been gone for four days."

"No. I only came out here this morning."

Then he thought about the mysterious house in which he had visited and eaten, how it had appeared and then vanished again, and while he thought that he had been away from home for only a day, his friends and relatives assured him that it had been four days. Then he knew that he had been with the Immortals.

Edohi had been in the forest four days. The ceremony would begin in three days and would last for four more. Edohi resolved that he would remain in the forest alone for at least seven more days. If anyone, Two Heads, Standing-in-the-Doorway himself or anyone else, should challenge him upon his return to Ijodi because of his failure to show up at the ceremony with his share of the game, he would say that he had spent a day with the *Nun-nehi*.

Somewhere in the West, the scribe *Kutani*, Iya-Iyusdi, Like-a-Pumpkin, alone, frightened and confused, was making his uncertain way back toward the country of the Real People.

Two

THE SPOILER tried not to think too much about her Shawnee slave, and when she did think about him, she tried not to give him a name. He was her slave, her Shawnee dog. She had hated the Shawnee people for years, ever since they had killed her husband, Tunai, the father of her two daughters. She had never remarried, and she had nurtured her hatred. When Edohi had brought this one to her, she had rejoiced. She would tie him in front of her house for all to see. She would make him work, and she would beat him now and then. And when she at last grew weary of his presence and was no longer amused by him, she would kill him in front of the whole town.

But she was beginning to think that she should have killed him right away, the day that Edohi had given him to her, for her hatred was softening toward the man. She had not considered the possibility that watching a Shawnee up close over an extended period of time, watching him eat and listening to him speak, would have such an effect on her feelings. She tried to remain hard and cold toward him, and she was at least managing, she was sure, to maintain that outward appearance. But inside she was growing soft, and that made her feel guilty. She felt as if she were betraying the memory and the spirit of Tunai. And the guilt made her angry.

The man had a handsome and dignified bearing, and he was polite and respectful to the Spoiler and to both of her daughters. And he was brave. He was not afraid to die. The Spoiler could tell that about him. In fact, he had seemed anxious to die when Edohi had first brought him to her. It didn't help any either that the man could speak the language of the Real People so fluently. She was softening toward him, and that made her angry at herself. So she decided that she would kill him that very evening. The whole town would watch, and then no one would ever suspect that her just and proper hatred for the Shawnees had ever diminished in any way. She would kill him in front of the townhouse, in front of all the people of Ijodi. The big ceremony was coming up soon. It might be a good time, she thought, for a killing.

Old Gone-in-the-Water crumbled tobacco leaves into a clay bowl with his wrinkled and leathery hands. He crumbled tobacco, *jola*, and he thought about the *Ani-Kutani*. From ancient times, the *Ani-Kutani* had been given charge of the public ceremonies of the Real People, the ceremonies designed to keep the worlds in balance and the Real People in harmony with all things. They also had charge of the old stories that explained why things were as they were and how the people should behave. Gone-in-the-Water had no problem with the ancient role of the priests. It did not conflict in any way with his own role as conjurer. His job was to deal with individuals on small matters, matters that concerned one person or a few. If a person was sick or hurt, that person would come to Gone-in-the-Water. If a person was having bad luck or had lost something or needed personal protection, Gone-in-the-Water was the one to be consulted. The roles were clear and did not conflict.

Gone-in-the-Water had heard the people complaining about the priests lately, but he had kept quiet. It was not a thing for him to get involved in. Secretly he agreed with them when they talked about the arrogant behavior of the *Ani-Kutani*. Those priests were no better than anyone else, certainly they were no better than Gone-in-the-Water. He was as good as any *Kutani*. He was sure of that.

But he had prepared those men for war that time, and the priests had interfered. In front of the people of his own town, they had stopped the men and said that they needed the permission of the head *Kutani*, Standing-in-the-Doorway. They had gone too far. They had stepped into his territory, invaded his realm, insulted his calling and questioned his integrity. Still he kept quiet. He stayed to himself. He crumbled tobacco into the bowl, and he thought about the *Ani-Kutani*.

The Outcast moved between the rows of corn. Most of the ears had already been picked, so he was finding but a few puny ones. Sohi, or Hickory Nut, the younger sister of Corn Flower, was picking beans. They were in the Spoiler's private garden, and there were other men and women working in the garden plot next to them. Sohi liked the Outcast. She hoped that her mother had decided not to kill her Shawnee slave after all. He was a handsome man with a pleasant disposition, although he did seem to carry with him a large burden of sadness. Sohi liked him. He was like a brother, she thought, an older brother. No. Perhaps an uncle. She wasn't sure, but she liked him.

She stood up to stretch, and when she did, she took a step back. A sudden, unmistakable, chilling sound came from behind her. The Outcast heard it too, as did the people in the neighboring garden. Sohi stood frozen, afraid to move, afraid even to look over her shoulder to try to find out how close *ujonati* was to her bare feet and calves. The Outcast spoke softly.

"Don't move," he said. He made a wide circle and approached Sohi slowly, cautiously, from her right side. It was not the biggest rattlesnake the Outcast had ever seen, but it came close. It was coiled, but it was standing up with its head as high as Sohi's knees. On the other end, the tail stood up straight and shimmered, singing its sinister song. The Outcast crept closer. "Don't move," he said again, his voice even softer than before. It seemed to Sohi that the Outcast was not even moving. It seemed to take forever for him to get close to her. But at last he did. Afraid to move, she rolled her eyes to the right. He was close enough to touch, and he was on his hands and knees. Slowly the Shawnee raised his right arm, and with his fingers widespread, stretched his right arm until it was between *ujonati* and the girl's bare legs.

"Now," he said in a barely perceptible voice, "step away very slowly."

She did, and when she was a safe distance, the Outcast began to move away too. He moved away as he had moved in, so slowly he seemed not to be moving at all.

"*Ujonati*," he said, "let's leave each other alone. Let's not meet each other again this year."

Sohi could hardly wait to tell her mother about the episode with the rattlesnake in the garden, but the Outcast gathered up all the corn and beans before they started back to the Spoiler's house. They put their baskets down by the door, and before the Spoiler could say anything, Sohi was talking.

"Mother," she said, "I almost stepped on a rattlesnake. I stepped back, and I heard his rattle, and I was this close to him. I couldn't move. I was so scared. He was big. The biggest rattlesnake I've ever seen."

"What did you do?" the Spoiler asked.

"I just stood there," said Sohi, "but the Outcast came."

The Spoiler turned on her slave. "Did you kill *ujonati?*" she said.

"No, Mother," said Sohi. "He came between *ujonati* and me, and he told me to walk away slowly, and I did."

The Spoiler put an arm around her daughter's shoulder, but she was looking at the Outcast.

"Sohi," she said, "go to your sister and see if she needs your help. I don't need anything more here. Go on now."

Sohi gave her mother a curious look, then glanced at the Outcast. She gave a little shrug, turned and headed for the house of Corn Flower. The Spoiler sat down wearily on the log bench beside her door. She kicked idly at the baskets of corn and beans which were there at her feet.

"You know," she said, "I was going to kill you today. I made up my mind."

"I'm ready to die," said the Outcast.

"No," she said, shaking her head. "No. You won't die today. Not by my hand. Not by the hand of anyone in Ijodi. You saved my daughter, Outcast. I've hated Shawnees for a long time, but I let you live too long, and now I know you, and now I'm in your debt for the life of my daughter. I can't kill you now, but I won't be indebted to you either. You're free, Outcast. You can go."

"I have no place to go."

"Then stay here. Do as you please. You're free."

"I would like to stay here, Spoiler," said the Outcast, "as your husband."

"Ha."

The Spoiler felt her face flush hot, and her mind tried to sort out a sudden confusing emotional rush. Other men had approached her over the years since the death of Tunai. None of them had caused much of a reaction. She had calmly and quietly rejected them all. Of course it had been pleasant to know that she continued to be desirable to the men, but that was only a mild response to their proposals. Perhaps in this case, she thought, it was the old hatred being aroused. Perhaps deep inside she was furious that a hated Shawnee would dare to make such a suggestion. Or perhaps, and her mind told her, more likely, it was anger at herself for not being outraged by the thought. He was handsome, bold and daring. He was a little younger than she, but what did that matter? He was everything a woman could want in a man, except, of course, he was Shawnee.

"Mother, Corn Flower's not at home."

The Spoiler was startled by the unexpectedness of Sohi's return.

"Oh well, she could be anywhere. There is still much to be done. Let's see what we have to do around here yet."

She tried to put the other thoughts to the back of her mind. She was glad that her daughter had come back to give her this reprieve. But what would she do come nightfall? She could no longer tie the Outcast to the front of her house to sleep outside like a dog.

Corn Flower had gone to the river. She was glad that there was so much work to be done. Staying busy kept her from missing Edohi quite so much. By the time the work was all done, the ceremony would begin, and Edohi would be back from his hunt. They would attend the four-day ceremony together, and then life would return to its normal routines. Things should be better even. If the priests were successful, it would rain, and the rain would make everyone feel better. She put down the clay vessel she had carried to the water's edge, knelt down, then turned to pick up the vessel again in order to fill it with water. A shadow fell across her, and she looked back over her shoulder. There stood Two Heads, a sardonic smile on his face. Standing to either side of him and a pace or two behind were two other priests, each young and burly, each with a stern, emotionless expression.

" '*Siyo*, old friend," said Two Heads. "Get up. You're coming along with me."

"Where?" said Corn Flower. "What do you want with me?"

"We're going to Men's Town. You've been selected to play a major role in the ceremony. Be proud. It's a great honor."

She stood, hesitated, then spoke.

"I'll just go tell my mother first," she said.

"Never mind that," said Two Heads. "She'll find out soon enough. Come along."

Still she hesitated, and Two Heads gestured abruptly toward his two husky attendants.

"Take her," he said. "Bring her along."

There were things in the bowl other than the crushed tobacco, and the old man plunged his hands into it and stirred the mixture. He sang some words as he stirred, sang softly. There was no one near to hear, yet he sang so softly that anyone sitting just by him would not have heard the words clearly. At last he stopped the song, removed his hands from the bowl and stood up.

"There," he said out loud. "It's done. Now I'll just get my pipe."

He turned around in a circle, looking as he turned.

"What have you done with it?" he said. "This is no time for your childish pranks. Oh, you. Where? You Little People. Ugly, where are you? Noisy? I'll kick you both out of here. You're going to make me lose my temper. Where—?"

His eyes stopped sweeping the room and focused there beside the small pot of glowing coals which stood in the center of his house. There beside the pot was his pipe.

"Ah," he said. "I scared you, did I? And so you put it back? Good. Good."

He picked up the pipe and carried it to the tobacco bowl to fill it. Then he moved back to the pot of coals and plucked out one small, glowing ember, dropping it into the bowl of his pipe. He poked the pipestem in between his age-puckered lips and sucked. Soon the rich smoke filled his little house. Again he muttered almost silent words, and with the backs of his hands, he wafted the smoke away from himself, toward the open door of his house, on its way to the road, in the direction of Anis-gayayi and the priests and their leader, Standing-in-the-Doorway.

Standing-in-the-Doorway turned to look as he heard the footsteps behind him. He saw Two Heads step into the room.

"I've brought her," said the younger man.

Standing-in-the-Doorway nodded slowly.

"Her robes are being prepared," he said, "and her special food and drink. All will be well."

Two Heads stammered before he could manage to speak again.

"I haven't—done anything else," he said. "I only brought her here."

Standing-in-the-Doorway stood and walked to Two Heads. He stepped close in front of him, facing him, and he put his hands on Two Heads's shoulders. Then he pulled the young man close to him and wrapped his arms around him. He held him close for a moment in silence, then released him and stepped back again.

"Go to her," he said. "Do as you will. It won't matter for the ceremony."

"Thank you," said Two Heads. His heart was pounding in his chest and his knees were shaking. The palms of his hands were wet and clammy. He turned to leave the room.

"Two Heads," said Standing-in-the-Doorway.

The young man stopped.

"Yes?" he said, and his voice was trembling.

"Come back here to me later," said the head *Kutani*, "after you're done with her."

Two Heads left the room, and Standing-in-the-Doorway stood quietly and alone. The day was coming to an end, and the light in the small room in the temple was fading to gray. He walked to the door and stared out at the evening sky. A great sadness which he could not define, could not account for, seemed to descend on him. Was it the drought? Certainly that was a contributor. But rain would come, sooner or later. He knew that it would. It always had. Another factor, he knew, was the general discontent of the people. But Standing-in-the-Doorway knew that he could handle the people. They were easy to manipulate. He knew that he could do what he wanted to do and tell them that he had done it for their own good. Their discontent would pass. What then? Was it this all-consuming passion, this obsession which held him in a death grip, this—love for the young man Two Heads? Perhaps. Of all the possibilities, that was the only one over which he could exercise no control. And Standing-in-the-Doorway had a deep-rooted need to be in control of everything around him. If anything ever gets the best of me, he told himself, it will be this passion.

Three

PEOPLE BEGAN TO GATHER outside Men's Town two days before the big ceremony was scheduled to begin. They constructed brush arbors and crude lean-tos for temporary shelter. Many of them were far from home. Everyone brought food, and there were cooking fires in front of most of the arbors. The next day almost everyone was there. The people from Ijodi, the closest town to Men's Town, greeted their clan relatives from Kituwah, Nikutsegi, Cheowee, Natli, Tellico and other towns from around the far-flung country of the Real People.

The pending ceremony was, of course, a solemn occasion, a desperate plea to the powers of the universe to send healing rains to a drying earth. In spite of that, the day before the ceremony was a festive one. Clans gathered together to visit. People caught up on the news from distant towns. A few spontaneous friendship dances were held out among the arbors.

From the dark doorway of his small private chamber in the temple, Standing-in-the-Doorway watched the activities with quiet satisfaction. Thus far, his plan was working. From all the dancing, feasting and visiting, it was obvious to him that the people had forgotten, for the moment at least, their dissatisfaction with the *Ani-Kutani*. Early in the morning, he would start the ceremony, and he would keep their minds distracted easily then for four more days. After that, well, if the ceremony worked, the rains would come. Then all would be well.

The Spoiler was near frantic with worry. Corn Flower was nowhere to be found. The Spoiler, Sohi, the Outcast, Stinging Ant, they had all been searching, and the friends and relatives they had questioned had also been looking. No one could find her. And Edohi had not returned. He was supposed to be back with the deer and the turkeys. He should be back. He should know about Corn Flower and be involved in the search. Finally, at her wit's end, the Spoiler had gone to War Woman, the powerful sister of Standing-in-the-Doorway.

"I don't know what to do," she had said. "This is not like my daughter. What should I do now, with the big ceremony about to begin?"

"I'll ask my brother," said War Woman.

So they waited. There was no place left to look, no one else to question. They waited. The Outcast sat in the dirt several paces away from the Spoiler. He knew that her mind was distracted with worry, and he didn't want to intrude. Yet he would stay near. If she needed him, if she wanted him to do anything, he would be right there.

Strange, he thought, how things had developed for him. He had been ostracized by his own people, cast out of his home. Then he had been captured by a young *Allegewi* man. He had wanted to die, but Edohi had refused to kill him, had instead taken him captive to Ijodi and made a gift of him to the Spoiler. Why? Since the Spoiler's husband had been killed by Shawnees, she had hated them all, and Edohi wanted her daughter, Corn Flower. So he had given her a Shawnee captive for a slave, and she, in turn, had given him permission to court her daughter.

The Spoiler had threatened to kill her new slave, and the Outcast had looked forward to the welcome death. But she had not killed him, and as time passed, his feelings for her had grown strong. Now he was free, but he could not go back to his own people. He no longer had any people. And he no longer wanted to die. Since the Spoiler had given him his freedom, he had continued to sleep outside her door. She had called him her Shawnee dog. Well, he would remain a faithful dog.

The Spoiler jumped to her feet when she saw War Woman coming, and the Outcast, too, got up and moved close enough to hear what was said.

"I've found her," said War Woman. "It's all right. You can relax."

"Where is she?"

"She's in Men's Town. She's safe."

"No woman is supposed to be inside of Men's Town," said the Spoiler. "Why is she there?"

"She's been chosen to take a special part in the ceremony," War Woman explained. "I heard it from my brother himself. You'll see her in the ceremony."

The morning began with a crier from Men's Town walking around outside the walls, in and out among the clutter of huts and arbors, calling for everyone to wake up and go to the river to start the day. The mass of people sorely challenged the diminished capacity of Long Person, but they crowded into his shallow waters and knelt, squatted or sat to splash themselves all over. Gradually they made their ways back to their campsites, cooked and ate. Soon the crier was back, calling out to them to give all their attention to the walls of Men's Town. The ceremony was about to begin.

It started with drums. Then rattles joined in. Then came the voices of the *Ani-Kutani*. One song followed another, and the songs were not songs that the people knew. They must be, the people whispered to one another, very old songs indeed. Certainly the *Ani-Kutani* possessed many old secrets. The people could not even understand some of the words in the songs the priests were singing. And the mysterious, sacred songs continued until the Sun had almost reached her daughter's house directly overhead in the center of the underside of the great Sky Vault. Then again the people cooked and ate.

When the meals were mostly finished, and the Sun was moving along toward the west, a *Kutani* came out of Men's Town carrying a platter on which cedar burned. He walked around Men's Town in a circle starting from the east and moving north. When he was done, four more priests came out, each one carrying burning cedar, and they walked among the people. Then the songs began again.

At twilight the singing stopped, and Standing-in-the-Doorway appeared on the wall. He called on Thunder to remember his friendship to the Real People, and he recited the story of how the friendship began.

A young boy of the Real People was out in the woods with his bow and arrows. He was hunting, but he had not had any luck, so he had wandered out farther and farther from the town in which he lived. He was down in a valley, and then he heard a tremendous commotion. He looked, and he could see, over the next mountain, that the turmoil was coming from there, from the other side. Great clouds of dust and debris rose up, and now and then whole trees were thrown up into the air.

The boy was frightened, but he was also curious, and his curiosity overcame his fear. He climbed to the top of the mountain to see what he could see, and there in the next valley, a furious battle was in progress. There was a man. He looked like a man, like one of the Real People. But perhaps he was not a man, for he was fighting a great *uk'ten'*, and the boy knew that no mortal could stand up to an *uk'ten'*. It was well known that the keen-eyed ones could kill with a look or with their fetid breath. And these two were locked in mortal combat, twisting and thrashing, tearing up great trees by the roots and flinging them up into the air. The boy was amazed.

In spite of the ferocity of their deadly struggle, the

combatants each saw the boy up on the side of the mountain.

"Boy," said the *uk'ten'*, "help me. Shoot this man, and I'll be your friend. I'll give you presents. Hurry up and kill him for me."

"Don't listen to him," said the man. "If you kill me, he'll turn on you. He can't be trusted. Shoot him instead, and I'll be your friend forever."

The boy thought for only a moment. The *ukitena* was ugly and frightening with his body like a giant snake, antlers on his great head and monstrous wings loudly beating the air. It was an easy decision to make. He nocked an arrow, and he shot the *uk'ten'*. It roared and thrashed its tail, but it did not die, and it continued to fight.

"Shoot him in the seventh spot," the man said. "That's the only place you can kill him."

The boy looked, and he saw that the *uk'ten'* had spots along the side of his huge body, and there were seven of them. He nocked another arrow and took careful aim. He let it fly, and it struck the *uk'ten'* in the seventh spot. It roared. It thrashed. It fell to the ground with a terrible crash, shaking the earth all around, and it died. And the man was Thunder.

Standing-in-the-Doorway finished the tale, and he prayed to Thunder to bring the rain. "Remember your friends, the Real People," he prayed. "Take pity on us in our time of need." When the prayer was finished, the first day of the ceremony was done. The people at their arbors or lean-tos ate or slept or visited. Far to the back of the crowd, alone, Gone-in-the-Water smoked.

. . . .

The second day was dancing, almost all of it. There were breaks, of course, but each was followed by more dancing. The Spoiler kept watching for Corn Flower, but Corn Flower did not appear. Neither did Edohi return from his hunt. The Spoiler knew that she was supposed to keep her mind on the ceremony and its purpose, but she couldn't. The absence of Corn Flower had been more or less explained, but not that of her son-in-law. The Spoiler's mind was distracted.

The third day passed with more songs, more dancing and more praying. Still the Spoiler did not see Corn Flower or Edohi. The Outcast watched her closely, aware of her worries and concerns, wishing that he knew of some way he could help. Toward evening a *Kutani* carried a pot of fire out of the temple on the mound inside Men's Town. The people gathered outside the walls could see the fire on the mound. Standing-in-the-Doorway spoke to them again. This was the perpetual fire, the sacred fire, the fire that never went out. He prayed again to Thunder, begging for rain, and the drums began to roll, imitating the rumbling sounds of Thunder just before a rain.

The Spoiler didn't sleep that night. She would see Corn Flower the next day, the final day of the ceremony, and she would at last find out what part her daughter would play. She was curious, anxious and, though she did not know why, apprehensive. Edohi had not yet returned, and she was worried about him. She also could not help but wonder if the ceremony would be successful and bring the rain. Then there was the matter of the Outcast and the astonishing proposal he had made to her. There were things more important to be considered, and she chastised herself for thinking about him, for giving serious thought to what he had said, for fantasizing about the things they might do together in the night should she decide to accept him.

She slept, or rather, pretended to sleep, beneath a hastily constructed arbor which the Outcast had put up for her outside of Men's Town. The Outcast slept in the open a few paces away. She had not yet invited him to come under her roof, and he had not pushed her. He stayed near. He did what he could to help. He waited.

This night, he waited as she waited, awake but pretending to sleep. He wondered if anyone among those gathered around Men's Town truly slept that night. He knew the language of the Real People well, and while people had not openly conversed with him, he had overheard plenty. He knew that there was widespread discontent among the Real People, knew that they had begun to doubt their priests, the *Ani-Kutani*. He surmised that the *Ani-Kutani* had revived this ancient ceremony to serve a twofold purpose: they were trying to bring the rain and break the drought, yes, but just as important, he figured, they were attempting to impress the people anew with their knowledge of old secrets and therefore with their own power and importance. This ceremony was as strange to the Real People as it was to him, an outsider. He had a sense that fate had brought him among the Real People at a momentous time, that important events were beginning to unfold. He tried to predict in his mind what those events might be, how they might develop, but he could not. It remained a vague but powerful foreboding. Nothing more. Nothing less.

Gone-in-the-Water, too, was awake. He sat on the ground to the back of the gathered multitudes, a small fire before him. He picked up his pipe and reached out with his right hand, touching the ground beside himself. He moved his hand. He felt around on the ground there to his right side. He looked. He turned to his left to look, and he felt around on that side. Nothing.

"Where is it?" he said. "Ugly. Are you here? Did you follow me over here? Noisy?"

He stood up with a loud groan, and bending over almost double, his face close to the ground, he turned in a circle, searching the area around himself.

"What have you done with my tobacco?" he said. "Where is it? Where have you hidden it? You Little People. You're worse thieves than Choctaws. Bring back my tobacco or I'll step on you."

He started to move around his small fire, shuffling his feet, kicking and grumbling. Then he felt something with his foot. He bent over to look, and he saw it there on the ground in front of him. He reached for it.

"Ah," he said. "You brought it back. It's a good thing, too. Good for you."

He sat down again right where he had been before, and he filled his pipe bowl from the tobacco pouch.

"Now," he said, "did you bring what I asked you to bring?"

The pipe pinched securely between his lips, he held

open the pouch down near the fire and squinted at it. He put the fingers of his right hand into the pouch and felt the tobacco. Then he sniffed his fingers.

"Ah, yes," he said. "You put it in there already. You mixed it in. Thank you, Ugly. Thank you, Noisy."

He folded the pouch over and laid it aside. Then he plucked a burning faggot out of the fire and lit the tobacco in the pipe. Puffs of blue-gray smoke rose from his mouth and from the bowl of the pipe to hover momentarily about his head before drifting lazily toward Men's Town, dissipating as they floated on their way.

The last day was almost done. The Sun was low in the western sky, not low enough yet for her light to have dimmed, but it would not be long. The people were all tired from four long days and little sleep. Priests danced in a circle around the temple on top of the mound. The Spoiler moved in as close as she dared. If she moved too close, she would not be able to see over the wall to the top of the mound inside the town. The sacred fire still burned in front of the temple. Then the song ended. The dancing stopped. Standing-in-the-Doorway stepped through the front door of the temple to stand just behind the fire, and he raised his arms over his head. He began to intone a prayer. It was a plea to Thunder to hear the prayers, to take pity on the people and on the land. Again he recited the story of the boy who shot the *uk'ten'*, and he reminded Thunder of what he had said that time. "I'll be your friend forever."

"And now," he said, "accept this offering, our gift to

you and to the sacred fire. Accept this sacrifice of the blood of the Real People and send us the rain."

Two priests came out the door, one on each side of Corn Flower. She was dressed in a beautiful feathered cloak, and she moved as if she were walking in her sleep. Even from her distance, the Spoiler could see that the expression on her daughter's face was blank, emotionless. What had they done to her? What were they going to do? Two Heads stepped from around the corner and held out at arm's length toward Standing-in-the-Doorway a large, two-edged, jagged flint blade. The two priests at Corn Flower's sides pulled back the feathered cloak until it slipped from her shoulders and left her standing naked, still expressionless, still motionless. The Spoiler opened her lips as if to scream, and Standing-in-the-Doorway's arm slashed upward, ripping open the bare breast, flinging blood, and the Spoiler's horrified, agonized shriek rent the still, hot, dry air.

Four

EDOHI CONSIDERED killing two deer and six turkeys and returning to Ijodi as if nothing was wrong, as if he were ready to go to Men's Town for the ceremony. If he had really been with the Immortals, he would not be aware of the passage of normal time, so he would let others figure out what had happened, draw their own conclusions. He imagined the scene that could take place.

"Edohi," they would say, "where have you been? We've been worried about you."

"Why, I've only been hunting, of course. See. I've brought these for the big ceremony, just as I was told to do."

"But the ceremony is over and done."

"It can't be," he would say innocently. "It was to begin tomorrow."

Then one would step forward, probably an old wise

one, perhaps Gone-in-the-Water himself, his face contorted by deep thought. "Edohi," he would say, "where did you go on this hunt?"

"I went in the forest. I went south for two days' walk, to the far edge of our country, and I met a man from a town over there. I'd never seen this town before. It must be a new one. I never heard its name. Anyway, he invited me to his home to eat. I ate with his family and then I left. I killed these animals, and then I hurried home to be back on time for the ceremony."

"Ah, Edohi," the old wise one would say, "you've been with *Nunnehi,*" and the faces of all those gathered around would register astonishment.

He thought that it would probably work out that way, yet in the end he decided against it. At least he failed to put it into practice. Perhaps he was simply uncomfortable with the idea of the falsehood. He felt lethargic. He lacked the will to hunt. The ceremony was surely over and done with, and he had not fulfilled his role, had not even attended the ceremony. Now he didn't feel like going home. He considered staying in the forest, taking up the life of a lone wanderer, but there was his family, and there was Corn Flower. He wondered if he could take Corn Flower and go away somewhere. But where? Could they live alone? Just the two of them? Live without the company of friends and relatives? It was a dreadful thought to one who had never known anything but the closeness of the town life and the security of the clan. Perhaps they could remove themselves to some remote town of the Real People. None of the Real People were totally removed from the all-powerful influence and authority of the *Ani-Kutani,* but there were some towns which were much farther away from Men's Town than was Ijodi. He wondered if Corn Flower would go with him to one of those towns. He wondered how the residents of such a town would receive them. He decided that he would propose such a move to Corn Flower just as soon as he could.

His mother would probably not like the idea, and surely the Spoiler would be opposed to it. But Edohi didn't think that he could stand much more of the arrogance of the *Ani-Kutani* and the haughtiness of Two Heads. He was afraid that if Two Heads dared ever so much as speak to him again, he might do some kind of violence to the priest. He might pull him by the nose or by an ear to the river's edge and throw him in, or throw him headlong down the side of a mountain. Or he might simply fling him to the ground, jump on him and pound him senseless. Well, he would have to talk with Corn Flower about moving away to some remote town. He could see no other way.

The Spoiler had to be dragged away from the walls of Men's Town by her friends. She screamed. She shouted threats. She fought them. Somehow they got her back to her own house in Ijodi. Everyone was stunned, and except for the loud protests of the Spoiler, Ijodi seemed to be a town in a trance. They had heard of such things from the distant past. They had never seen it, never expected to. There was very little talk in Ijodi that night. But the morning was different. People had slept, or not, but the night had passed, and they began to talk.

"Did you ever think to see such a thing?"

"No. Of course not."

"Will it work? Will it bring rain, do you think?"

"I don't know."

A small group of women were huddled together in front of a house talking in harsh whispers.

"Do you think that it's right, the way the Spoiler is carrying on so?"

"What do you mean? She's lost her daughter. How should she behave?"

"When one has been chosen for a special role in a major ceremony and is privileged to give her life for the good of all, that is not a thing to be mourned. It is a thing to be proud of."

"Ah, I don't know. Perhaps you're right. If it had been my daughter—"

In another part of town, members of the Bird Clan sat together, somber.

"What will Edohi do, do you think," said Beavertail, "when he finds out what has happened?"

"I don't know," said Wild Hemp. "I'm afraid to think what he might do. He'll be crazy with grief."

"Just as are we all," said Hemp Carrier. "Crazy with grief and anger. Who would have believed that even Standing-in-the-Doorway would go so far? To take a man's wife? To kill a young woman? One of our own people. He has gone too far this time. Too far."

"Well, brother," said Wild Hemp, "control yourself for now. And when my son comes home, control him, too, if you can. I must talk to the Spoiler, but not just yet. She has to have some time."

• • • •

He did not know how far away from home he was. He wondered how much longer he would have to travel. He looked hard at the landscape around him as he moved east, trying in vain to recognize something, anything from the time he had come through before, heading in the opposite direction. But he wasn't even sure that he was retracing his steps. He was going east. More than that he could not say. He did know, or at least he felt fairly certain, that he had gotten well beyond the territory of the fierce people who had captured him and his two companion priests, who still held Deadwood Lighter and who had killed poor Water Moccasin.

Poor Water Moccasin. Like-a-Pumpkin sat down heavily on the ground. He had been running long and hard, running for his own life, trying to make his way safely back home to the land of the Real People, and he had not had the leisure to give much thought to the fates of his two unfortunate traveling companions. He and the other two priests had left Men's Town, it seemed so long ago, with instructions from Standing-in-the-Doorway to go west, to find the house of Thunder and to bring back the rain. But they had been captured by a strange, fierce people who had made them slaves, had beaten them unmercifully and had kept them on leashes like dogs. Water Moccasin had made a foolish break for freedom, and they had killed him. And Deadwood Lighter? Like-a-Pumpkin could only assume that Deadwood Lighter was still a captive, still a slave of the fierce people. But Like-a-Pumpkin had bided his time, had waited for the right moment, and then he had used the rabbit's trick to escape. Then he had headed for home.

And only now with the time to sit and think did Like-a-Pumpkin realize the horrible worst of all that had happened. Water Moccasin's remains had been left alone, neglected, far from home, victim to the ravages of the weather and the appetites of scavengers. The spirit of Water Moccasin must be very unhappy, perhaps hopelessly lost. The body should have had a proper burial at home. It should have been washed and wrapped and laid on a scaffold for a period sufficient for the flesh to decay. Then it would have been taken down. The bones would have been cleaned, then laid to rest properly inside the temple at Men's Town. Instead it had suffered the opposite, had received the worst treatment imaginable for the remains of a man of the Real People. Considering at long last the miserable fate of the soul of his former companion, Like-a-Pumpkin suddenly shuddered convulsively. He looked up toward the great Sky Vault, opened his mouth and released a long and anguished wail. And when the wail at last subsided, he wept.

Finally, emotionally spent, Like-a-Pumpkin stood up. He was naked except for the oversized breechclout and moccasins he had taken from the body of the man who had been his tormentor, the man he had killed in order to escape. He picked up the weapons he had also taken from that man, the bow, four arrows and the jagged flint knife he had used to deal the death blow. He faced east, and he started walking. He had not eaten for some time, and he was hungry, terribly hungry. His stomach cried out for food with each step he took. Up ahead, a rabbit darted out from behind a clump of brush and stopped, its nose twitching. Like-a-Pumpkin fitted an arrow to the bow and took aim. The rabbit song came into his mind.

Ha nia li li.

He hesitated, then lowered the weapon.

"No, Jisdu," he said. "I won't kill you."

He stood still and watched the rabbit. It ran a short way and stopped again. Like-a-Pumpkin followed at a respectful distance. The rabbit ran again, stopped again. Like-a-Pumpkin followed. He followed it out into an open field, and it stopped there in the midst of a thick blanket of green. Then while he watched, it began to eat. Like-a-Pumpkin eased up closer. Jisdu had led him to a patch of wild lettuce, *igosdi agisdi*, and it was green and plush. There must be water somewhere near, Like-a-Pumpkin thought. Perhaps it was underground. Well, he would not question a gift. He moved a little closer.

"*Wado*, Jisdu," he said, his voice low and gentle. "*Wado*. That's twice now you've saved my wretched life."

He crept closer, and soon, at opposite ends of the same patch of wild lettuce, Jisdu and Like-a-Pumpkin, their noses twitching, were grazing away.

Around Men's Town things were deathly quiet. Standing-in-the-Doorway lifted a gourd cup to his lips and drank greedily. He had drunk much water that day, more than usual, much more. Yet his lips felt parched, and his throat was dry and dusty. It was the dusty air, he told himself. He just couldn't seem to get enough water. But it was more than that, and he knew it. He had revived the ancient ceremony and performed it fully, and the sky was still clear, the air still hot and dry and dusty. Standing-in-the-Doorway stared off toward the west, toward the home of Thunder, seeking in vain some sign, however slight, that relief was coming. But he saw nothing. He heard no distant rumbles. He felt nothing in the air but dry dust.

And he had killed the young woman. He could get away with it, he knew, if the rains would only come. But if they did not, the people would rise up against him. He had known the desperate chance he was taking, and he had made the decision to go ahead. He alone. And why? Because he believed that the old ceremony, including the ultimate sacrifice, would bring the rain? Perhaps. Or perhaps it was simply the greatest imaginable gamble. He had never seen the ceremony performed. No one living had. How then could he have known anything about its effectiveness? He took a chance. He gambled. And of course, Two Heads had wanted the woman. He had done it, at least in part, for Two Heads. He could have, he supposed, waited a little longer for the return of the three priests he had sent to the west.

"Ah, Two Heads," he said in a scarcely audible whisper, "what would I not do, what would I not risk for you?"

All, he thought, silently responding to his own question. I have risked it all. He dipped himself another cup of water and drank it down. I fear, he heard himself thinking. I fear the end. The end is approaching. He wondered how long he could delay it. Everything has an end. Even the world will die someday. But one can fight, and sometimes one can hold off the inevitable—for a time. And then again perhaps this heavy sense of dark foreboding was not an accurate prediction of the future. Perhaps after all the rain would come. He could not be sure.

He walked back into the room and stood for a moment, allowing his eyes to adjust to the darker interior, staring toward the cot where Two Heads lay sleeping. Then he walked across the room, knelt beside the cot and gently laid a hand on the young man's bare shoulder. The smooth flesh was sticky with sweat, gritty with salt and dust. Two Heads stirred. He lolled his head over and opened his eyes. He smiled and reached out, putting an arm around the shoulders of Standing-in-the-Doorway.

"I want you to do something for me," said Standing-in-the-Doorway. "It's something of utmost importance."

Two Heads sat up on the cot.

"I'll do anything," he said.

"Get some men to help you. Spread the word around that the rains will come in seven days. The ceremony must be observed for four days. It was. Seven days later it will rain. During that seven days, the *Ani-Kutani* fast and pray. Spread that word among the people."

"Do we fast?" said Two Heads. "I've eaten already since the ceremony."

"No one outside of these walls needs to know that," said Standing-in-the-Doorway. "This seven days is to keep the people quiet. It's to buy us time."

"Will it rain?" asked Two Heads.

"Pray that it will," said Standing-in-the-Doorway. "Now go. Do as I told you. In seven days the rains will come."

He watched the young man stand and slip on his robe,

then leave the room. He sat down on the cot and leaned back against the wall.

"Or it will be the end," he added. "One thing or the other."

The Outcast had helped the Spoiler retrieve the body of her daughter from the spot where it had landed after the priests had flung it over the wall at the ceremony's end. He had wrapped it carefully in the skin of a deer and carried it back to Ijodi. The Spoiler's mind had been distraught. She had cried and wailed and cropped her hair, so Stinging Ant, though he too mourned, had to tell the Outcast what to do. They took Corn Flower to her own house and laid her out inside. Some of her clanswomen came and washed her and wrapped her up again, and then the Outcast, according to instructions from Stinging Ant, built a scaffold not far outside of town and placed her there. Then they burned the house. There would be nothing more to do for a while, nothing except to wail and to cry. And that was what the Spoiler did. She sat on the ground in front of her house, her short hair disheveled. She scraped up handsful of dirt and dropped the dirt over her head, rubbed it into her hair. She wailed. She wept.

The Outcast sat nearby, and he, too, wept, but though he wept openly, he wept silently. He wept for the lost Corn Flower, and he wept for the agony of the Spoiler. He felt helpless, and he wanted more than anything to be of help. But what could he do for her? What could anyone do? Was there any loss worse than the loss she had suffered, the loss of a child? Children were expected to have to endure the funerals of their parents. The opposite was both unexpected and unnatural. He longed for a way to comfort the Spoiler, but he knew that there was no way, that she would simply have to go through this sad and angry period of mourning. So he would do as he had been doing. He would stay nearby, and he would wait, and for now, he would help her mourn.

Two Heads found four apprentice priests and told them what Standing-in-the-Doorway had said.

"After the four-day ceremony, we fast and pray for seven days. Then it will rain," he said. "Go out into the towns and tell this to the people."

When the four left Men's Town, Two Heads stood alone beside the wall just inside the entryway, and he started to cry. The sudden sobs and tears surprised him at first. He did not know why they had come upon him. He had hated Corn Flower, he reminded himself. She had spurned him and insulted him. She had humiliated him that day she threw him in the river. Even before that, back when they had been childhood playmates, she had always tried to show him up. He was a boy, and she was a girl, yet she could outrun him. She was a better hunter than he was. And that time the Choctaws had captured them, she had been brave, and he had been afraid. For as long as he could remember, she had demeaned him, not by anything she said, but by her actions, and he hated her. Well, he had gotten even. He had his way with her, no matter that she had been drugged stupid by powerful herbs, and she was dead.

Why then did he feel so hollow, so empty? Why did he feel—guilty? Why did he miss her so? He wiped his eyes with the backs of his hands, took a deep breath, resolved to think no more of her, and headed back toward the temple.

Five

GNAT WAS SMALL, even for his eight years. They said that even at birth, he had been a tiny baby, and his mother's "little grandmother," her grandmother's sister, had said, "He's as tiny as a gnat," and they had called him that ever since. They said that he was like his uncle, his mother's brother, Like-a-Pumpkin, except that he was not so ugly. Gnat didn't think of Like-a-Pumpkin as ugly, though. Like-a-Pumpkin would have been the one to raise Gnat up in the ways of a man of the Real People, to teach him to hunt and to fight, to discipline him when it was called for, but Like-a-Pumpkin had been taken away from them. He had been called to the life of a priest and had gone to live at Men's Town. They seldom saw Like-a-Pumpkin after that, and the duty of training and disciplining Gnat had fallen to Mink, his mother's other brother, really her clan brother, her mother's sister's son. But Like-a-Pumpkin was not often out of Gnat's young mind. Gnat longed for the infrequent visits of his favorite uncle, and he admired the man's good-natured, often funny ways.

Gnat was only eight years old, but he heard the grown-ups talk. He, like everyone else, knew that the Real People were suffering from a drought. He knew that his favorite uncle and two other men had been entrusted with a very important mission. They had been sent to find the house of Thunder to bring back the rain. He also knew the *Ani-Kutani* had given up for lost Like-a-Pumpkin and the other two. They had gotten tired of waiting and had held the big ceremony in which they had killed the woman. Gnat had been there. He had seen the ceremony, and he had seen the woman killed. And he had not said anything to anybody, not even to his mother, but he knew in his heart that the priests were wrong. The ceremony was unnecessary. The woman had died for nothing. He knew that, because he knew that his uncle would succeed. He knew that Like-a-Pumpkin would return, and when he did, he would bring the rain.

Gnat sat quietly and alone on a hillock outside of Kituwah, the town in which he lived. He sat there staring off toward the west, expecting at any moment to see the familiar, funny figure of Like-a-Pumpkin appear in the distance, trudging toward him, smiling, rain clouds billowing behind him, his approach heralded by deep, resonant rolls of thunder. It was hot, and it was dry, but Gnat didn't mind. He anticipated relief. He knew that he would soon be drenched with fresh, cool, sweet rain, and he knew that it would be following Like-a-Pumpkin. He could endure the drought, knowing what he knew. He was patient. And soon, he thought, everyone would know what he knew, and everyone would have to recognize the worth and the accomplishments of his uncle. Gnat was looking forward to that.

The boy had begun this daily vigil the day that he had heard about the ceremony, and since then, he had watched every day. Even during the ceremony, he had found moments to steal away alone and watch. He felt the *Ani-Kutani* had betrayed Like-a-Pumpkin, and no one else seemed to realize that. He alone remained faithful. And so he sat, and he watched.

Edohi came walking over the hill. He was not in a hurry. He did not really want to be back home in Ijodi, but he had put it off as long as he could, he had decided. He was going back to Ijodi, but he was not pushing himself. He was taking his time, and he was going through Kituwah first. He would stop and visit and waste some time in Kituwah. The Bird People, his clan relatives, in Kituwah would make him welcome. They would feed him and put up with him for as long as he chose to stay. The road to Kituwah was at the foot of the hill, and Edohi trotted down to it. Puffs of dust rose up from the dry road as his feet pounded onto it. He slowed back down to a walk, and then he stopped as he noticed a figure up ahead. The figure didn't move, so Edohi resumed his walk. Soon he was close enough to see that it was but a boy, and the boy was just sitting there.

" *'Siyo, 'chuj',*" said Edohi, as soon as he was close enough for words.

" *'Siyo,*" said the boy.

"I'm Edohi of the *Ani-Tsisqua* from Ijodi."

"I'm called Gnat," said the boy. "I belong to *Ani-Waya*, the Wolf People, in Kituwah."

"Do you mind if I sit here with you?" Edohi said. "I've been walking a long ways today."

"No. I don't mind."

Edohi sat down beside Gnat and looked with him toward the West.

"Is someone out there?" he asked.

"My uncle," said Gnat. "I'm waiting for him to come back."

"I see," said Edohi. "Where has he gone?"

"He's gone to the West," said Gnat, and before he realized what he was doing, he added, "to find the house of Thunder and bring back the rain."

"Ah," said Edohi, nodding his head. Everyone knew about the three priests who had been sent west. "He's a *Kutani*. Which one is your uncle?"

"He's called Like-a-Pumpkin."

"Oh, yes. I remember him. He's a ball player, too, isn't he? I saw him play once against the Choctaws."

"I was just little then," said Gnat, "but I remember it. They beat the Choctaws."

"Yes. They did."

"And my uncle played well that day."

"Yes," said Edohi. "He made the winning point. He was good."

"He's coming back," said Gnat.

Edohi knew that the priests had been given up for lost. Otherwise there would have been no reason to hold the big ceremony. He was sad for Gnat, sitting and staring west, waiting for the return of his uncle, who was probably dead somewhere in the unknown West.

"Will you sit here like this," he said, "until he returns?"

"I come out here every day for a while to watch."

"Have you watched long enough today?"

"I guess so," said Gnat, and Edohi could hear the disappointment in the young voice.

"Then will you walk with me into your town?"

"Yes."

They stood up and walked together to Kituwah, but just as they were about to enter the town, Gnat stopped.

"Edohi," he said.

"Yes?"

"Don't tell anyone what I was doing."

Edohi looked down at the boy, at the big, nearly black eyes which rolled upward to look at him for a pleading instant, then looked away again.

"I won't tell anyone," he said.

They walked on in, and Edohi accompanied Gnat to the boy's house. A woman was cooking on a fire in front of the house. She looked up at the approach of Gnat and the stranger.

"That's my mother," said Gnat.

" '*Siyo,*" she said. "I'm Walnut."

Just then a man stepped out of the house, obviously curious to see who it was who had come to visit.

"And this is my husband," the woman continued. "He's called Rock Thrower."

"I'm Edohi. I just met your son outside of town. I'm on my way home. I live at Ijodi."

"You're welcome to eat with us," said Walnut.

"*Wado*," said Edohi. "I was just going to look for my relatives, the Bird People."

"Ah," said Rock Thrower, "I'm a Bird Person. Come on. Sit down."

There was no more talk until they had all eaten, but soon after, they were talking about the ceremony. Everyone, Rock Thrower said, was talking about the ceremony.

"Were you there?" he asked Edohi.

"No. I was in the forest. I—couldn't get back in time. I'm only now on my way back home."

"You're the only person I've talked to who wasn't there," said Rock Thrower. "Have you heard about it from someone else?"

"You're the first people I've talked to since the ceremony took place. I haven't seen anyone else."

"It was like nothing we've seen before," said Rock Thrower. "It lasted four days."

"Everyone was there," said Walnut. "Even people from Nikutsegi. There were songs we'd never heard before. Dances we'd never seen."

"The people from all over were camped out around Men's Town, and the priests sang from up on the walls. They danced all the way around Men's Town. A big circle."

"Standing-in-the-Doorway, himself, prayed from up on the wall where everyone could see him and hear him," said Walnut. "He prayed every day. But the last day was when the big surprise came."

"A big surprise?" said Edohi.

"Yes," said Walnut. "It was awful, but I suppose the priests know best about these things."

"They brought a young woman out of the temple," said Rock Thrower. "She was wearing a feather cape, and when they took that off of her, she was naked. Then Standing-in-the-Doorway cut her open and pulled out her heart."

"What?" said Edohi.

"Blood was everywhere," said Walnut. "It was awful."

"Then they threw her body over the wall, and the ceremony was done," said Rock Thrower. "No one expected it. No one had ever seen anything like it. They said that it was an old ceremony which Standing-in-the-Doorway revived because of the drought. It was the last thing to try to make it rain."

"It hasn't rained," said Edohi.

"No," said Rock Thrower. "Not yet. Standing-in-the-Doorway says that we have to wait for seven days after the ceremony. Then it will rain."

"Do you believe it?" asked Edohi. "Will the killing of this woman bring rain?"

"I don't know." Rock Thrower shrugged. "When Selu saw that her own two boys meant to kill her because they thought that she was a witch, she told them to go ahead. 'Then drag my body seven times in a circle,' she said, 'and you'll have corn enough to eat in the morning.' They killed her, but they got tired of dragging the body. They didn't drag her seven times. So now our corn takes a long time to grow, but it's only because of her blood, our Corn Mother's blood, that we have corn at all. Maybe this sacrifice will bring the rain. Maybe. I don't know."

"Who was the young woman?" Edohi asked.

Rock Thrower shook his head.

"I don't know," he said. "A young woman. Very beautiful."

"A captive?"

"No. She was one of us. One of the Real People. I remember Standing-in-the-Doorway said the sacrifice was our own blood. She was one of us."

"It was awful," said Walnut.

"She didn't suffer," said Rock Thrower. "They had given her something, I think. Something to drink or something to eat. I don't know. But I don't think that she knew what was happening. I don't think she felt anything either."

"Still it was awful," said Walnut. "I don't think they should have done it. I guess they know best, but I don't believe it will work either."

"I agree with you," said Edohi. "They shouldn't have done it. And killing a woman is not the way to make it rain."

Like-a-Pumpkin stopped. There before him was the big river, the one the naked people had carried him and his companions across in their dug-out canoes. But this time Like-a-Pumpkin was alone, and he did not see the village of the naked people on the other side. He had apparently arrived back at the big river either farther north or farther south than where they had crossed before. Without the help of the naked people, he couldn't think how he would be able to cross. He sat down to think, but all his mind seemed to want to tell him was that he was hungry. He stood back up and walked toward the river. Perhaps he would find something to eat growing along the edge. Near the water, he stood still for a moment, looking around for any possible danger. Then he hopped over some rocks and looked again. He saw no one. Working his way north along the riverbank in short jumps, he at last came to a small patch of wild turnips, and he knelt down to eat. He ate the greens and he ate the tubers. He ate until his belly felt swollen, and he drank from the running river. Then he lay back to rest and to think.

He had solved the immediate problem of hunger. The next problem was how to cross the river. He looked in both directions, trying to remember, trying to decide which direction to take to find the village of the naked people, those friendly and generous people who had helped him and his companions when they had been traveling west. If he could find the naked people, maybe they would help him cross again.

A rabbit appeared a short distance away, to the right of Like-a-Pumpkin. It seemed to look at him, its pink nose twitching.

" '*Siyo*, Jisdu," Like-a-Pumpkin said. "If you want some of these turnips, I've left plenty for you."

The rabbit didn't accept Like-a-Pumpkin's offer. Instead it turned and hopped farther away from him, going south. It stopped and faced him again, watching. Like-a-Pumpkin stared back at the rabbit, curious about its behavior. It turned and hopped farther away and disappeared, but in a short while, it returned. It was watching Like-a-Pumpkin again. Then it came to Like-a-Pumpkin that the rabbit was trying to get his attention, was trying to lead him somewhere. He thought it was probably a crazy idea, but then, there was no one around to witness his foolishness, no one besides Jisdu. He got to his feet and walked toward the rabbit. It turned and raced away, but just when Like-a-Pumpkin thought he was about to lose it, it stopped, and it seemed to be waiting for him to catch up.

In just that manner, Like-a-Pumpkin followed the rabbit for some time. It continued south, and it stayed close to the river's edge. Then suddenly it veered west and raced away. Like-a-Pumpkin started to follow, shrugged and sat down. He felt foolish, but, he repeated to himself, there was no one around to see him, and he was no worse off than he had been before. He had just about begun to believe that he had found an ally in Jisdu, that the great trickster rabbit had decided to look after him. After all, something had put the story of the rabbit's escape from the wolves into his mind at just the right time, and he had been able to escape from the fierce people by imitating the rabbit, by singing his songs and dancing his dance. And a rabbit had led him to the wild lettuce when he was hungry. Was it such an outlandish thought, then, to think that rabbit was consciously helping him? Had it been foolish to follow this rabbit along the river? He wasn't sure.

He had heard the story of rabbit's escape from the wolves hundreds of times in his life, had repeated it almost as many. Of course it would come back into his mind at a time when he was in desperate need of an escape plan. And the other one, the rabbit that led him to the lettuce, perhaps it had just been going to the lettuce, and Like-a-Pumpkin had cleverly followed it. This latest one had certainly led him nowhere, if it had been leading him at all. So how was he going to cross the river? And where was the village of the naked people?

Six

STANDING-IN-THE-DOORWAY knew deep in his secret thoughts that he was not perfect. He might fool others, but he did not fool himself. He also felt a secret twinge of guilt for the way in which he had selected the woman for the sacrifice. Even so, there was nothing in his training or in his studies that had prescribed the way in which the victim was to be selected. It had been his choice, his decision. It seemed to him that so long as the ceremony had been properly conducted, it should matter little how or why the victim had been chosen. And he had conducted the ceremony with great care. It had been perfect as far as he could tell. Why, then, his thoughts roared in his head, was it not raining?

He had dreamed up the seven-day fasting and praying period to keep the people from asking out loud that same question. They would wait quietly, he thought, the seven days. But Standing-in-the-Doorway already knew that something was dreadfully wrong. He hoped for rain at the end of the seven days, but it was only a hope. He had done everything he knew how to do. It should be raining already. Perhaps the end was really approaching. It seemed to Standing-in-the-Doorway that ends were often overseen by great men. Perhaps that was to be his destiny, to preside over the end of the world.

He was standing on the temple mound staring west as these thoughts wandered aimlessly in his head, veering this way and that, dodging one another adroitly, occasionally colliding with one another. He looked over to the wall where a young priest was standing guard. He only had to raise his voice a little to be heard.

"You on the wall," he said. "Find Two Heads and send him to me."

He didn't watch to see that his command was being obeyed. He knew that it would be. He walked to his private chamber door and stepped inside. The room seemed black except for the broad spots of light that danced before his eyes, grew larger until they exploded and were replaced by smaller spots that in turn grew, exploded and were replaced. He had stared too long at the bright sky. He blinked his eyes, trying to make the light spots go away. He didn't even notice when Two Heads stepped inside to stand beside him.

"You sent for me?" said Two Heads.

"Yes," said Standing-in-the-Doorway, the abruptness of his response betraying a little his surprise. "Take me to the cot."

"Are you ill?" asked Two Heads.

"No. Not ill. My eyes are not accustomed to the darkness of the room. That's all."

Across the room, he dropped his cloak to the floor and with a heavy sigh, stretched out naked on the cot. Two Heads knelt beside him.

"You're tired," he said.

"My body is weary," said Standing-in-the-Doorway.

Two Heads began to massage the older man's feet.

"Ah, that's good," said Standing-in-the-Doorway. He paused, trying to relax under the pressure from the young hands, the kneading of the smooth fingers. "It should be raining now," he said.

"But the seven days haven't yet passed," said Two Heads.

"The seven days was made up for the benefit of the people," said Standing-in-the-Doorway. "I made it up. The rain should have followed the blood. It should be raining now." Two Heads's hands were on the head priest's calves, stroking the skin, kneading the muscles. "Something has gone wrong," Standing-in-the-Doorway continued. "I performed the ceremony just as it should be done. I did everything. I left out nothing. Someone somewhere has done something wrong." He paused again as the young priest's hands crept up to his thighs. "Or someone has failed to do something he should have done. Otherwise it would be raining now."

Two Heads's hands stopped moving. He stared for a moment at the wall, stared in deep thought.

"Edohi," he said.

"What?"

"Edohi," said Two Heads. "He used to be called Sparrow. He was the other one with me that time we first met."

"Yes," said Standing-in-the-Doorway. "I remember him."

"He was supposed to kill two deer and six turkeys and bring them for the ceremony. He didn't do it. He didn't bring them. He didn't even show up to attend."

Standing-in-the-Doorway reached down and took Two Heads by both of his wrists, then drew him upward until the young man's hands rested on his own chest. Then he slid his own hands up Two Heads's arms until they reached his shoulders. The flesh was gritty.

"Then this Edohi is to blame," he said. "He is the cause of all our troubles." He sat up on the cot, suddenly feeling renewed. "Get us some guards," he said. "We'll go to the river and bathe, you and I. Then I'll have to decide what to do about this Edohi."

Like-a-Pumpkin sat where the rabbit had left him. He was still wondering how he would cross the river. He thought that he might find a log to hold on to and paddle his way across like a dog. But he wasn't at all sure that would work. He didn't see a good-sized log anywhere near, and besides, his body would be in the water, and he still wondered what kinds of creatures might live in this river. Something might come up from the depths and eat his legs. Then he heard a shout. He was lounging in a slight depression, so he scrambled to its edge and peered cautiously over the rim. A canoe was in the water coming from the other side. Two men were in the canoe, one paddling, the other struggling with a small boy. On the opposite shore, a naked man danced in apparent anger and frustration, shaking his fists and shouting after the canoe. The man rowing the canoe laughed. The boy screamed, fear in his voice, and struggled with the other man. Like-a-Pumpkin watched in silence as the boat drew nearer to the western shore.

The men in the boat were painted. They had stolen the boy, Like-a-Pumpkin decided, from the naked man on the other side. Then he recognized the boy, and he thought that he could also recognize the man across the river. They were the father and son of the family of naked people who had befriended him and his companion priests and then helped them to cross the river on their trip west.

"*Wado*, Jisdu," he said. Then he looked again at the two painted men in the boat, and he added, "I think."

Like-a-Pumpkin had never been a warrior, but he could shoot an arrow, and he had killed an enemy. Keeping down, he nocked one of his four arrows and waited. The boat drew nearer. The boy still struggled, but with less conviction than before. The bottom of the heavy dugout canoe scraped the ground, and the man in front jumped out, dragging the boy after him by his arm. The boy twisted and jerked, almost pulling himself free, and the man shouted at him and cuffed him hard across the face.

The other man was in the water wading to shore. He wasn't bothering to pull the boat up. Apparently he didn't care if it drifted away. He had probably stolen it along with the boy. But Like-a-Pumpkin cared. He needed the canoe. He stood up and drew back the bowstring, taking careful aim, and he let the arrow fly. An instant later, it buried itself with a sickening thud in the chest of the oarsman who had just stepped out of the water. The man looked down at the quivering shaft protruding from his flesh, his eyes wide with horrified surprise. He fell backward, landing in the shallow water in a sitting position, his legs out straight in front of him, then slumped forward for a moment, then slowly fell over to one side.

The boy took advantage of the shock and jerked his arm loose and ran. The man made a motion as if to go after the boy, paused, looked at Like-a-Pumpkin, then made his decision. He let out a fearful shriek and ran directly toward Like-a-Pumpkin, who was fumbling to nock a second arrow. Only two or three strides away from Like-a-Pumpkin, the man made a mighty leap. Like-a-Pumpkin screamed, dropping bow and arrow, and put up his hands in an attempt to protect himself from the hideous, painted figure hurtling through the air, coming at him, warclub in hand. The man's left hand caught Like-a-Pumpkin by the throat, but Like-a-Pumpkin's two hands, palms out, pushed against the other's chest. Even so, the weight and force of the man carried Like-a-Pumpkin over onto his back, but as he fell, he brought both feet up and planted them in the man's belly. As he landed on his back, he straightened his legs, and the other flew head over heels, screaming. He hit hard on his back, two body lengths away from Like-a-Pumpkin. Somewhere in flight, he had lost his warclub, and the air had been knocked from his lungs on impact with the ground. Flat on his back, he sucked hard for air. Like-a-Pumpkin moved quickly, pulling loose the flint knife that hung at his waist. He ran to the fallen man, dropped to his knees at the man's head and plunged the dagger into his heart. Hot blood spurted out onto Like-a-Pumpkin's hand. The man's legs kicked, his throat rattled, his eyeballs rolled and he died.

Like-a-Pumpkin sat back on the ground panting. His heart was pounding hard in his chest, just like, he thought, the heart of a frightened rabbit. Then he remembered the boy—and the boat. He jumped to his feet and looked around. The still frightened boy was standing off at a safe distance. The boat was slowly drifting away from the shore.

"Get the boat," Like-a-Pumpkin shouted, and realizing that the boy couldn't understand his words, he pointed frantically. The boy got the message. He ran to the boat, waded into the water, pushed the boat out farther and jumped in. Then he began paddling furiously for the opposite shore.

"Wait," shouted Like-a-Pumpkin. "Wait for me."

But, of course, the boy did not understand. Like-a-Pumpkin sat down dejected. Oh well, he had saved the boy at least. And he couldn't really blame the youngster. He had just had a terrible fright, and he couldn't know whether Like-a-Pumpkin intended to rescue him or steal him from the other thieves. He probably hadn't recognized Like-a-Pumpkin. There was too much excitement, and Like-a-Pumpkin was no longer dressed in his priestly robes. So he still had to find a way to cross the river, but first things first. He checked the bodies of his two victims, taking their moccasins and weapons and breechclouts. They had nothing else of value to him. They had not carried bows and arrows, but each had a warclub and a knife. He took off the moccasins he had been wearing and looked at them. They were badly worn, with holes in their bottoms. He tossed them aside and put on the pair he had taken from the feet of the man he had knifed. The other pair was wet. Then he glanced up, and he saw the canoe coming back across the water. The boy was still in it. His father was rowing.

The Spoiler was done with mourning. Now she was angry. She wanted revenge. She wanted to restore the balance that had been disturbed by the killing of her daughter. The proper way was to kill either the killer, Standing-in-the-Doorway himself, or any member of his clan. But the Spoiler knew that satisfying the clan law would not satisfy her rage. With no one else near, she lashed out at the faithful Outcast.

"Why did they take my daughter away from me?" she said. "To make rain? Where is the rain? And what has the blood of my daughter to do with rain?"

"I don't know, Spoiler," said the Outcast. "I wish I could answer your question, but I don't know your ways."

"No one knows our ways, apparently," she said. "I thought that I knew the ways of the Real People as well as any, but I have never before seen such a thing. None of my neighbors has ever before seen it. You know as much as anyone else."

He stood quietly by, unable to think of anything to say, feeling helpless, wishing he could do something for her. He didn't like seeing her this way. He understood her pain and her rage, but he longed for the passage of time, which alone, he thought, would heal her wounds.

"There is no rain," she said. "Look." She scooped up a handful of dry dirt from between her feet and held it out in front of her to blow away in the warm wind. "The world is dry underneath our feet. It blows away. It's dry everywhere except at Men's Town where it's wet with the blood of my daughter. And look at the sky. Do you see any clouds? Do you see any sign that rain is coming?"

"No, Spoiler," said the Outcast. "I see no sign of rain."

"And where is my worthless son-in-law?" she said. "He should be here. He should know about this. His wife has been killed, and he doesn't even know about it. He should be here. He should be doing—something."

"Spoiler," said the Outcast, relieved at last to discover something he could do, "I'll go find Edohi for you and bring him back."

And it turned out to be even easier than he had thought it would be. He had no idea where to look. Edohi had gone hunting. That was all that anyone knew. He could have gone in any direction, and he had been gone so long that he could be just about anywhere. The Outcast went out of town by the passageway in the wall. No one bothered him or challenged his right to wander free and alone. All of the residents of Ijodi had become aware of his new status, of the freedom that the Spoiler had given him, and no one would challenge her right to bestow it.

Outside town, the Outcast left the road almost immediately to climb the mountain there. Halfway to the top, he looked around, and he saw Edohi. He was walking toward Ijodi, coming from the direction of Kituwah. He brought no game. He was not in a hurry. The Outcast, watching him amble toward home, believed that Edohi was not aware of what had happened during his absence, and he realized that in volunteering to go fetch Edohi for the Spoiler, he had placed himself in the uncomfortable position of having to break the awful news to Edohi. "Ah," he said to himself, "how will I tell him?"

Edohi had fought with the Outcast, overcome him, brought him to Ijodi as captive, all because of his strong feelings for this woman, and now the Outcast was to inform him of her death. Ah, well, he had made a promise. He started down the mountainside toward the road to meet Edohi there.

Seven

E DOHI."

"'*Siyo*, Outcast, my old friend," said Edohi. He stopped walking and stood in the road facing the Shawnee who was there blocking his way. "Have you come to get your revenge? Are we going to fight again?"

"There was a time when I would have welcomed the chance to fight you again, Edohi, but not now. Though I would rather fight you than do what I have to do."

"What?" said Edohi. "What are you talking about?"

"Not here in the road," said the Outcast. "Walk with me to some place more private."

Edohi shrugged. The Outcast was behaving in a most peculiar manner, he thought. Perhaps he was planning to trick Edohi, to lead him off the road and attack him by stealth. But Edohi didn't really believe that. The Outcast was a proud and bold warrior, and if he wanted to kill Edohi, he would announce the fact openly and defiantly.

So it was something else. Edohi walked with him. They left the road and climbed the low mountain there outside of Ijodi, the same mountain from which the Outcast had observed Edohi on the road. They climbed to its crest, and then they sat down on a large boulder there. They looked down to their right on the town, and to their left the road stretched out below until it wound around a mountainside and vanished from their sight on its way to Men's Town, Kituwah, eventually the Choctaw country. The view was stunning. It would have been beautiful were it not for the deathly dryness, and it would have been totally dismal with the dryness, were it not for the life-giving waters of Long Man, the Tanasi, winding their way through the desolation. They sat for a long moment in silence, surveying together the thirsty landscape.

"You stayed away for a long time," said the Outcast.

"Yes," said Edohi. "I'm thinking of leaving this place."

"Where would you go? Would you become a wanderer, an outcast, like me?"

"There are towns of the Real People far from here. Remote towns. If I went to one of those towns, I would never have to—"

Edohi paused and stared out across the dry expanse.

"Yes?" said the Outcast.

"I'd never have to see the priests again."

"You can't escape them in your own country, Edohi. At the big ceremony for rain, they said that people were there from every town of Real People. They said that almost everyone was there, everyone who could travel, everyone—except Edohi."

Edohi stood up and walked a few paces away to stand

with his back to the Outcast. He gazed toward Men's Town.

"Edohi," said the Outcast, "have you heard about the ceremony? Have you talked to anyone who was there?"

"I stopped in Kituwah," said Edohi. "Some people there told me about it."

"They told you—everything?"

"You mean the sacrifice?" said Edohi.

"Yes."

"They said that Standing-in-the-Doorway killed a young woman of the Real People to make it rain. Ha. I see no rain."

"Edohi."

Edohi still stared toward Men's Town.

"Edohi, it was your wife."

Edohi turned to face the Outcast, his face registering both horror and disbelief.

"What? What did you say?"

"It was your wife that was killed by the *Kutani.*"

Edohi reacted as if he had been kicked in the stomach. He doubled over, and the air was loudly expelled from his lungs. He stared at the Outcast in pain and dread. Then a low wail began to escape from his lips. It grew gradually in intensity until it had become a painful howl, and when Edohi's lungs were exhausted and depleted, and the howl had died in a few painful, gagging gasps, Edohi pulled out his flint dagger and raised it high, holding it in both hands, the deadly tip pointed toward his own breast.

"*Hlesdi,*" the Outcast shouted, and he simultaneously sprang into action. Flinging himself at Edohi, he grabbed the younger man's forearms just below the wrists. Edohi struggled to free himself from the Shawnee's grip.

"Let me go," he said.

"Drop the knife," said the Outcast.

"No."

They pushed against each other and twisted, Edohi trying to break loose from the powerful grasp of the Outcast, the Outcast desperately trying to keep Edohi from plunging his knife downward. Their feet were firmly planted. Their upper bodies strained from one side to the other. Then, as if by mutual agreement, the two opposed bodies flung themselves to one side, landing heavily on the ground. The impact jarred loose the Outcast's grasp on Edohi's arms, and Edohi rolled quickly away. Flat on his back, he again aimed the knife at his own heart. The Outcast, still on his back, spun and kicked, and the knife flew out of Edohi's hand and off to one side beyond easy reach.

Edohi rolled over quickly and scrambled on his hands and knees toward the knife, but the Outcast reacted just as quickly, turning and leaping onto Edohi's back, and Edohi collapsed under the force. He stretched out his right arm, but the knife was still beyond his reach. The Outcast grabbed Edohi's flowing scalplock and pulled, then reached under with his left arm, locking it around Edohi's neck. Edohi gagged and choked.

"Stop fighting me," said the Outcast.

Edohi struggled just a little more, then he relaxed. The Outcast released his hold on Edohi's head and neck. He still sat on Edohi's back.

"Let me up," said Edohi. "Leave me alone. I want to die."

"The last time we fought," said the Outcast, "I wanted to die, and you wouldn't allow it. But now all you have to do is listen to me. Then I'll go and leave you alone, and you can do whatever you want. Will you listen?"

"Yes," said Edohi.

The Outcast stood up, releasing Edohi. He walked over to where Edohi's knife lay, picked it up and handed it, hilt first, to Edohi. Edohi took it, stood up and sheathed the weapon.

"Say what you have to say," he said, "and then leave me alone."

"Don't you *Allegewis* mourn your dead?"

"Of course we do."

"If you act in haste and kill yourself in your grief, you won't have done so. Mourn properly for your lost wife. Then kill yourself if you still want to."

Edohi's body started to shake, and he began to sob. Then he unleashed another long and loud wail. The Outcast waited for it to end before he spoke again.

"Both your family and your wife's family have been looking for you," he said. "You're not alone in your grief, so even though it won't be easy, you need to think of others. Not just yourself."

Edohi sucked in several long, deep breaths of hot, dry air.

"You're right, of course," he said. "I'll be all right. At least for now. Can you show me where— Where—is she?"

"Come with me," said the Outcast, and the two men began their descent of the mountain together.

· · · ·

The naked people remembered Like-a-Pumpkin, but they were obviously puzzled by his appearance and by the fact that he was traveling alone. They wondered, apparently, what had happened to his companions, to his clothes, to his mission. He tried his best to understand their hand sign questions and to make them understand his responses, but he felt they had understood, at best, half of what he tried to tell them.

They fed him, though, fed him well, but Like-a-Pumpkin discovered to his own surprise that he was losing his taste for meat. He ate a little of what was offered, but he filled himself with beans, potatoes and greens, especially greens, and his nose twitched as he ate. His hosts again gave him a place to sleep, and the following morning they gave him provisions for his trip. He was better provided than he had been since leaving Men's Town, but he was still reluctant to leave the village of the naked people. They were generous and friendly, and it seemed to Like-a-Pumpkin that he had been a long time without such human company. Yet he had to resume his journey. He had to get back home and report the failure of his mission. The thought of having to present that information to Standing-in-the-Doorway was almost enough to make him linger longer there with the naked people, but his strong sense of duty prevailed. He bade his hosts farewell and started, once again, walking east.

It seemed to Like-a-Pumpkin that the whole world lay between him and his home. Even starting out from Men's Town with only a vague western destination, he had not felt so overwhelmed by space and distance. But then he had not been alone. He felt incredibly small and insignificant. He suffered from a sense of hopelessness and dread, and he wondered if he would ever see his home, ever again hear spoken his own language.

Then he saw the rabbit. It was almost in his path, and it was looking at him. Like-a-Pumpkin stopped and stared.

" '*Siyo*, Jisdu," he said.

Of course, the rabbit made no verbal response. It stared with large eyes back at Like-a-Pumpkin, and it twitched its nose. It seemed to Like-a-Pumpkin to be scolding him with its look, chastising him for his lack of resolve.

"You're right," he said to the rabbit, and it turned and ran. I'm not alone, he thought. Jisdu has been with me all the while, and I've been very fortunate. I escaped from the fierce people. I even killed my captor, Black and Red. I found food. I killed the people who were stealing the little boy, and the naked people helped me once again. I'm alive, free, well, and I'm not alone.

"*Wado*, Jisdu," he said out loud. "Wherever you are, Jisdu, thank you."

He walked on, still conscious of the long trek and the possible dangers ahead, but in much lighter spirits than before. And he considered Jisdu, what he meant to the Real People, his characteristics, his habits, the lessons he taught. An enigmatic figure, the rabbit, in the tales told by the Real People, could be foolish or wise. He seemed always to think that he could do anything. Sometimes that worked to his advantage, as when he escaped from the wolves, but often it had been his own foolishness and arrogance that had gotten him into the trouble in the first place.

There was the time, for instance, he boasted that he could swim in the water and eat fish just as the otter did.

"Prove it, you braggart," said the others.

"I eat ducks, too," said the otter.

"Well," said the rabbit, "I eat ducks, too."

"Let's go see," said the otter.

So they went to the river, and they walked along its edge until they saw some ducks out on the water. They sneaked along carefully to get as close as they could without being seen or heard.

"You go first," said Jisdu.

The otter slipped into the water and swam underwater, so the rabbit couldn't see what was going on, but soon one of the ducks just vanished under the water. The otter had come up under it and pulled it down. The other ducks didn't even notice. Pretty soon the otter with his duck reemerged at the bank of the river where Jisdu waited.

"See," he said, holding up his duck by its feet. "Now let's see you try it."

While the otter had been swimming underwater, Jisdu had peeled a strip of bark from a nearby sapling and fashioned a noose at one of its ends. Now he held the coiled strip behind his back out of the otter's sight, and he looked smug.

"Try it," he said contemptuously. "Ha. I'll do it."

And he jumped in with a splash. Under the water, he paddled desperately with all four feet, but in just a little while, he was out of breath. He came up to the surface gasping for air, coughing and choking. He sucked in a deep breath and went back under. This time he made it to the ducks, and he came up in their midst. The frightened ducks quacked, fluttered their wings and started to fly, but Jisdu acted quickly and threw his noose over the head of the nearest duck. Then he tried to go back under with his prize, the way the otter had done, but the duck, more powerful in the air, rose up. Hanging on to his rope, Jisdu rose up, too.

The duck flew higher and higher, and the rabbit, looking down, was afraid. He gripped the bark rope as tightly as he could, and he watched in horror as the ground below seemed to fly beneath him. Then, tiring, he lost his grip, and he began hurtling toward earth with a scream.

But luck was with Jisdu, for down below was a hollow, standing tree stump, and Jisdu fell straight down inside. But it was a tight fit, and the hole in the top was the only hole, so there was no way out. Jisdu was stuck. He yelled for help, but there was no answer. He tried to climb up to the hole at the top of the stump, but he couldn't do it. When it grew dark, he was still there in the stump, and he was hungry. The rabbit was in big trouble, and it was all due to his own foolish bragging.

The next day, Jisdu was very hungry. He was so hungry that he ate his own fur. He was getting desperate. Then, late in the day, he heard the voices of children playing, and he started to sing.

> Cut a door and look at me.
> I'm the prettiest thing you ever did see.

The children ran away, but before long they came back. They had brought their uncle with them, and the rabbit sang his song again. The man cut a hole in the stump down close to the ground, but it was too small, so Jisdu sang some more.

> Cut it larger.
> Cut it bigger.
> I'm as pretty as I can be.

The man made the hole a little larger, and he and the children gathered around to look into the stump. Just then the rabbit jumped out, startling them, and he ran away. So he had gotten himself into trouble by being foolish, but once in trouble, he got himself out of trouble by his cleverness.

I've been foolish, too, from time to time, thought Like-a-Pumpkin, but with Jisdu's help, I'm still alive. I'm free. I'm all right. But, he reminded himself, he had to be careful not to become too confident, not to be cocky. Jisdu sometimes seemed to think that he really could do anything anyone else could do. Like-a-Pumpkin recalled the story of the time Jisdu had moved into a new neighborhood.

Everyone was real friendly. The beavers cut down trees, and the bear stacked them up to build Jisdu a house. Everyone helped. And when they were done, the bear, knowing that the rabbit hadn't had time to store any food in his new house, invited him to supper. At bear's house, bear was cooking, but he needed more grease. He took a knife and sliced himself along his fat side and held a bowl under the fresh cut to catch the drippings.

A few days later, with food in his own new house, the rabbit decided to repay his friendly neighbor and host. He invited the bear to eat. When bear showed up, Jisdu started to cook. He needed some grease, so he took a knife and cut himself in the side, but nothing came out but blood. The bear put the hurt rabbit to bed and went outside to call the neighbors. He told them what had happened.

"We need a doctor," he said.

The buzzard showed up just then.

"I'm a doctor," he said. "Wait out here, while I go inside and see what I can do."

Jisdu's neighbors paced back and forth in front of the house. Now and then they heard Jisdu squeal. Then the bear called out to the buzzard.

"How is he?"

"Oh, he's good," said the buzzard.

"Can we come in and see him?"

"No. Not yet."

They paced some more, and eventually the buzzard came out of the house.

"How is he?" said the bear.

"Oh, you can go in and see him now," said the buzzard, and he spread his great wings and lifted himself into the air. The others crowded into the house as the buzzard flew away. Inside they found the rabbit's bones.

And this, thought Like-a-Pumpkin, was his helper. He had to think of all of the rabbit stories to understand the lessons they taught. Never give up. That was one lesson. But be patient and wait for the right time. That was another. But finally, don't be too cocky. No one can do everything. It's important to be aware of one's limitations. Surely that was a big lesson.

Eight

THE IMMEDIATE ANGUISH over the death of Corn Flower passed. It was slowly replaced by a numb emotional ache accompanied by a seething anger. The Spoiler was changed utterly. She began every morning by wailing publicly. She neglected her hair and her overall appearance, and her face wore a constant hard and cold expression. People, even her best friends, tended to avoid her for fear that her fuming ire might happen to erupt in their presence.

But the Outcast stayed always nearby, always within easy reach of her voice. If she should need him, he would be there. He would be there to provide, within his power, anything she might want. He himself had become an accepted fixture around Ijodi. Some people walked past him without seeming to notice his presence. Others spoke to him as they passed by, and some had even begun to stop and visit with him. He had come into the town a prisoner, a hated enemy, but it was known that the Spoiler had granted him his freedom, and the Spoiler's right to do that was respected.

Sohi, who had been so full of life until the death of her sister, had become quiet and contemplative. She went about her daily tasks slowly, quietly, methodically. If anyone tried to engage her in conversation, she answered, if at all, in barely audible monosyllables. Other members of both clans were affected in similar ways to varying degrees.

But Edohi stayed to himself. After the Outcast had escorted him to the platform on which the remains of his young wife rested temporarily, and he had gone into town to see his family and hers, Edohi had faded into the background of life in Ijodi, or he stayed outside the walls, in the woods, or up on the mountaintop. Of course, for a long time Edohi had spent more time away from town than in it, so his absence was not particularly unusual. But Edohi wasn't hunting. He was just staying to himself, sitting alone, brooding in his misery. If only, he thought, I had acted sooner on my idea of leaving this place. Or if I had stayed in Ijodi instead of going out for so long pretending to hunt.

Corn Flower was supposed to have been sacrificed in order to bring rain. Edohi considered that, and he thought of the story about the hunter whose wife had killed a rattlesnake. The hunter had been surrounded by rattlesnakes immediately thereafter, and the chief rattlesnake had given him a choice. Go home and send her outside where the rattlesnakes could kill her and have their revenge, or they would kill the hunter right then and

there. The hunter had gone home and sent his wife outside to die. The idea of sacrifice for some purpose was not
unknown to him. Edohi couldn't decide if he was wrong
or right, but he knew that he would never knowingly have
sacrificed his wife, nor would he have stood by and allowed others to do so had he known. He was confused, he
was in deep grief, and he was bitterly angry.

There were some in Ijodi who stood by the *Ani-Kutani*.
Turning against all they had ever known, everything they
had ever been taught, was too much for them. They were
a minority, and they had begun to keep more and more to
themselves, visiting in small clusters, speaking low and
conspiratorially. A few of the women were working in the
gardens, and they noticed that they were all of a mind.
There were no representatives of the opposing point of
view within earshot.

"Have you noticed the way the Spoiler has been behaving?" said one.

"Ha," said another. "Who could not notice? Cutting
her hair short. Throwing dirt all over herself. Neglecting
her appearance all of this time. Wailing every morning for
everyone to hear."

"And that Shawnee hanging around her like a faithful
dog. It's shameful."

"Her daughter was chosen by Standing-in-the-Doorway himself. She gave her life for a good cause, for the
good of all of the people. The Spoiler should be proud.
She shouldn't be grieving in public the way she's doing. It
isn't right."

"It could keep the ceremony from working. It could keep us from getting rain."

"It isn't right, what she's doing."

"She's one of those who've been questioning the authority of the *Ani-Kutani* all along. She and her family."

"And her new in-laws. The family of her son-in-law, Edohi. That Hemp Carrier is one of the worst."

"He's certainly the loudest. Something ought to be done about them."

"But what? There are too many of them here in Ijodi. They outnumber us by far."

"Perhaps someone should go to Men's Town and tell the priests what's happening here. Perhaps someone should do that before things get any worse."

Like-a-Pumpkin was not confident of his way until he found the road. He had walked up a hillside, and when he reached the crest, he saw it there on the other side. He had figured that if he traveled in the right direction generally, eventually he would stumble across it, and that was just what he had done. There had been times when his spirits were down and he had doubted his strategy. He had thought that he might be doomed to endless lonely wandering, but he had kept going through these bouts with depression, and he had made it. He had found the road.

He started down the hillside slowly, but he picked up speed as he moved, partly because of the downhill grade, partly because of his own anxious elation. By the time he made the bottom of the hill, he was running, and he ran on out to the middle of the road. He stood there, and he turned around in a circle, surveying his surroundings. Yes. It was the road. It was the right road. He recognized that very rock on the south side, and now that he was standing in the road itself, he recognized the hillside he had just descended. He even thought he recognized one tall oak tree. He had found the road. He laughed out loud with joy. Then, because there was no one else around to talk to, he talked to himself.

"I've found it," he said. "I've found the road. I'm home. I'm back. I made it."

Gradually his words established a rhythm, and then a tune evolved, and he was singing a new song. Then he was singing and dancing there in the middle of the road.

> I made my way.
> I found the road.
> I'm on my way back home.
> I killed the nasty Red and Black,
> and now I'm going home.

He wore himself out singing and dancing, and he sat down to catch his breath. When at last he was breathing easily again, he stood up.

"Ah," he said, "that was foolish. Had someone happened along the road, he would have thought he'd found a fool. Ah, well."

Yes, he realized, he certainly would have looked a fool, but, of course, it could have easily been worse than that. He reminded himself that even though he had at last found the road that would eventually lead him right back to Men's Town, he was not yet in his own homeland. He was not at all sure just whose land he was in. He knew that he would have to travel through a bit of Chickasaw country and then through Choctaw country before he would be safe, and then he thought about the Chickasaws he and his companions had encountered early in their westward journey. The Chickasaws had reluctantly allowed the three priests to go on their way unharmed, only because they were going after the rain. And what was it the one Chickasaw had said to them? "When we see you coming back, if it has not rained, we will kill you then." Something like that. The unknown dangers were behind him, but, Like-a-Pumpkin told himself, there were still plenty of known dangers, well-known dangers, on the road ahead.

Following these sobering thoughts, Like-a-Pumpkin looked around himself once more, this time warily. He did not want to have to fight for his life. He was a scholar-priest and not a warrior. It was true he had killed before, three times now. Even so, just thinking back to those incidents still made him shake with fear. With Black and Red he had been desperate, and he had used trickery. And at the big river, he had shot the first man from ambush without warning. He had actually fought the other one, but he couldn't even remember what he had done. It had all happened so quickly, and he had reacted out of fear and panic, and he had somehow prevailed. He might not be so lucky the next time. Water Moccasin had been the warrior-priest of the three, and look at how he had wound up. Poor Water Moccasin. Like-a-Pumpkin shuddered. He would do everything he could to avoid contact with any human beings until he was confident that he was well within the boundaries of the land of the Real People.

. . . .

The seven days had come and gone, and then some people from Ijodi had visited Men's Town. Hoping they would go away, Standing-in-the-Doorway had made them wait outside the wall for a long time before he had gone down to see them. He had been afraid that they had come to complain, that they would question him about the passage of the seven days without the promised rain, that they would accuse him of having slaughtered one of their own to no purpose. But when at last he had deigned to present himself to them, they had not said those things. They had come to him as informers against their own townspeople. Ijodi, they had said, was on the verge of revolt. The mother of the young woman who had been sacrificed was openly wailing and mourning and shouting out for everyone to hear such things as "Where is the rain? And what did my daughter die for then?" In the end he had thanked them for their loyalty, commended them for their bravery and sent them home with instructions: continue to do as you have done, act as spies, keep me informed. Then he had gone back to his private chamber, where Two Heads was waiting.

"We are rapidly approaching a crisis," he said. "The people of your town are almost ready to take up arms against us."

Two Heads, naked on the cot, sat up startled.

"They wouldn't dare," he said. "How could they?"

"We killed one of their daughters," said Standing-in-the-Doorway. "We did it to bring rain. It did not rain, so we said that it would come in seven days. The seven days have passed, and still there is no rain. There is no sign of rain."

"But you've done everything," Two Heads protested. "You sent those three to the West, and you revived an ancient ceremony. What do they want? What do they expect of you?"

"They expect results," said Standing-in-the-Doorway. "They want rain."

"It's Edohi's fault," said Two Heads, springing to his feet and going to Standing-in-the-Doorway. "He didn't attend the ceremony. He didn't hunt, the way he was supposed to. He didn't do his part. Edohi's to blame."

Standing-in-the-Doorway reached out and put a hand on Two Heads's cheek. He slid it around to the back of the young man's head, then pulled the head gently down onto his own shoulder and held it there for a moment. Then he released Two Heads and paced away. He stopped in the doorway and stared out at the unrelenting sky.

"Yes," he said. "Edohi. Put on your robes, Two Heads. Go out and get some warrior-priests. Only two. Two should be enough, I think. Send them to me. Then find your tattlers. The same ones you used before to spread the word about the seven days of fasting and prayer. Send them out again. This time to spread the word that the ceremony has failed, and it failed because of this Edohi."

Nine

THE SPOILER of the Deer Clan talked to Wild Hemp of the Bird Clan. Each in turn talked to all the other women in her own clan in Ijodi, all except the few who were known to remain loyal to the priests. Some of them went to talk to women of other clans. Soon just about every woman in Ijodi had been contacted, and the few who were loyal to the priests were somehow aware that they had been left out. They were not at all sure of what they had been left out of, but they knew that they had been left out of something.

"They are plotting against us," one said.

"They are plotting against the *Ani-Kutani*," said another.

"They wouldn't dare," said yet another. "They are just grumbling together."

Then representatives of the seven clans, the plotters, went out to other towns. They went first to Kituwah and the other towns that were within easy reach, and they talked with their clanswomen there, and women in those towns went to other towns. There could not be a major, formal gathering. They would have to consult with each other in this somewhat more awkward manner, but in only a few days, a surprisingly short period of time, the Spoiler, Wild Hemp and five other women of Ijodi, one from each clan, met again. They met at the Spoiler's house. The Outcast stood outside watching.

"Are we all agreed?" asked the Spoiler.

"Yes," said Wild Hemp. "The *Ani-Kutani* must be utterly destroyed."

The others all muttered or nodded assent.

"What are they saying then," said the Spoiler, "in the other towns? What will they do?"

"No one will stand in our way," said the representative of the Wolf Clan. "Some people from towns nearby said they would help us. Some few said they would simply stay home and mind their own business. They are mostly from the farther-away towns."

"There are some, even here," said the woman from the Long Hair People, "who are against us. If we're going to do anything, we'd better do it soon, before they find out what we're up to and warn the priests."

"They already are suspicious," said the representative of the Blue People. "Some of them have already gone to Men's Town, I think."

"They know that we've been grumbling and complaining," said the Spoiler. "I don't believe they know we're planning anything."

"What will we do about these people?" the Wolf woman asked.

"We won't kill them," said the Spoiler, "unless they join in the fight on the other side."

"But what if they do join in?" asked the Blue woman. "If we kill them, we could start a war of clan revenge."

"The seven clans are all represented in Men's Town anyway," said the Long Hair woman. "It won't make any difference."

"We have to agree," said the Spoiler, "that after the priests are all dead, no one will seek revenge for any clan. No one. That Two Heads, for instance, is a Bird person from right here in this town, as is my friend here, Wild Hemp. Will the Bird People take revenge for the death of Two Heads?"

"No," said Wild Hemp. "We will not. For these present purposes, we will not consider him to be a Bird Person. He is only a *Kutani.*"

"Can we all agree to this?" said the Spoiler.

They all agreed.

"Good," said the Spoiler. "Spread that word throughout your clans. Now it is time to tell our men, and they can plan the attack."

He saw them well ahead standing across the road. Had they known he was coming? Had they been watching him? He couldn't be sure, but he thought they were the same Chickasaws who had promised to kill him and his companion priests if they should return without having brought the rain. He didn't think that they could possibly recognize him from that distance, even if they were the same people. They had seen three robed priests. He was returning one man alone in breechclout, carrying weapons. Even so, they did not appear to be friendly. He thought it would be good if he could keep them from getting any closer to him than they were already. To his left was a river valley. To his right a mountain, rocky and tree-covered, rose sharply. The river could be a death trap. He turned and started moving toward the mountain, and he saw the five Chickasaws come running toward him on the road.

He ran. He ran for the mountainside and for the cover of its trees. The Chickasaws ran after him. Like-a-Pumpkin reached a large oak, and he stepped around behind it. The naked people had given him a good supply of arrows, and he thought that one might be well spent here to let his pursuers know that he would fight and to slow them down a bit. He nocked an arrow and let it fly, not bothering to take careful aim. Just let it come close. Slow them down. It buried itself in a Chickasaw's thigh. The man yelped in pain, stumbled and fell. The others gathered around him for a moment of uncertainty. Then, leaving one behind with the wounded man, three of them resumed the chase, but Like-a-Pumpkin was out of sight in the trees.

The way soon became too steep for running, but Like-a-Pumpkin continued to climb as fast as he could. He knew there were still three men in pursuit of him. He knew that they no longer had him in sight, but he also knew that in the forest anything could happen. He couldn't see them either. He could come across his pursuers or they him totally by accident. He stopped for a moment to listen, and he could hear them below, yelling and crashing through the brush. He hurried on.

He was winded by the time he reached the top, but he knew they were still coming. The ridge ran roughly parallel to the road and was relatively free of trees and brush. He began to run along the ridge, running still east, running at a comfortable, easy lope. Every now and then he turned and, trotting backward, watched his back trail. He did not see them coming. Had they given up, or were they still back there somewhere? He had no way of knowing.

He could keep running along the ridge and eventually back down to the road and hope that he could outrun them, or he could dodge back into the trees in an attempt to evade capture. He rejected the latter idea as too uncertain and too time-consuming. But the first idea didn't seem much better. Like-a-Pumpkin had never been much of a runner. He was afraid that he would tire, slow down and be caught. The third alternative was to stand his ground, meet them face to face and fight, but he rejected that one without giving it any serious thought. He decided he would run, but he had to have more of a plan than that. He wondered what Jisdu would do in this situation, and then he realized again that there was more than one way to learn from Jisdu. Jisdu sometimes learned his own lessons the hard way, but others could take advantage of Jisdu's hard-gained knowledge.

Jisdu got in a race one time with Dagasi, the terrapin. Dagasi was a strong warrior, but he was boastful, and Jisdu got tired of listening to him brag.

"Well," he said, "one thing for sure you can't do is run fast."

"I could beat you in a race anytime," said Dagasi.

"Ha."

"Let's arrange it then. For tomorrow."

They planned the race for the next day. They would race across four ridges. All the other animals were invited to watch, with some being posted at the fourth ridge to be the judges at the finish.

"This is ridiculous," Jisdu said. "I'll beat you too easily. It's hardly a race. I'll start at the first ridge while you start at the second. I'll give you that much of a lead to even things up a little, but I'll still beat you badly."

Dagasi shrugged his unconcern.

"Whatever you say," he said.

Jisdu went home to sleep, but Dagasi went to find two other terrapins, friends of his who looked just like him. He told them his plan, and the next day when it was time to start the race, Jisdu was ready at the first ridge. Ahead on the second ridge, the terrapin, barely visible for the tall grass, was ready. But it wasn't Dagasi. It was one of his two friends. The other friend waited on top of the third ridge, and Dagasi himself was hiding in tall grass on the fourth ridge very near the finish line.

The race was started, and Jisdu ran down the side of the first hill and up the side of the second hill to the second ridge. He was running easily, and he laughed as he sped by the slow-moving terrapin. Going down the second hill and up the third, he didn't bother running even as hard as before. He knew that he was so far ahead he didn't have to hurry. But as he approached the second ridge, he saw the terrapin there ahead of him. It astonished him so, he nearly fell over.

"How did you get here so fast?" he said, but he didn't wait for an answer. He raced ahead. Going as fast as he could up the side of the third hill, Jisdu was getting tired. He got close to the ridge, and then he saw the terrapin there. He could scarcely believe his eyes, and he couldn't imagine how the slow terrapin had once again gotten so far ahead of him. Now he ran harder than ever. He started down the hill running so hard that he tumbled and fell headlong and rolled all the way to the bottom. Scampering to his feet, he started up the last hillside toward the fourth ridge and the finish line.

He was almost there, but he was gasping for breath, and his heart was pounding ferociously. He looked up, and there on the ridge, crossing the finish line, was Dagasi. Jisdu fell over on his back.

"*Mi mi mi,*" he said. He was trying to get his breath. The race was over. He had lost.

Now there's a lesson in there somewhere, thought Like-a-Pumpkin. He glanced over his shoulder. There was still no sign of his pursuers, but he noticed that he was leaving clear footprints on the dry ground of the ridge. He slowed his pace to a walk and wandered close to some brush cover to his right. Then he walked out away from it again, searching the ground ahead for a path less likely to leave obvious prints. He located an area covered with rocks and clumps of dry grass, and he stepped into it, causing his trail to disappear. Anyone following him would keep going straight ahead hoping to pick up his trail again somewhere farther along the ridge. Then he began to walk backward, carefully stepping into his own footprints. He backed up that way until he was once again near the brush cover, and he jumped into it. Concealed in the brush, he looked out to check the effectiveness of his ruse. He could see his own tracks leading right past him to fade away up ahead. He settled down to wait.

He didn't wait long. The three Chickasaws came following his trail. They were running, and as they ran past him, he could hear them talking to one another in short, quick phrases. They paused for a moment where his tracks disappeared, then pointed ahead and ran on. His trick had worked. He let them get well ahead, then he emerged from the brush and followed.

He didn't try to catch up with them. He didn't want to take a chance on being seen. He tried only to keep them in his sight. But they were moving fast. They must have been convinced that he was still ahead of them, and they were hurrying to catch him. He wondered how long they would run after him without catching sight of him before giving up the chase. He wondered what he would do when they did give it up.

They kept up their fast pace for most of the rest of the day. Now and then they would stop to look for tracks. Then, finding none, they would again race blindly ahead. Like-a-Pumpkin stayed well behind them, close to brush, in shadows when possible, but he kept the Chickasaws in sight. And then they stopped. The ridge had trailed off, and they had run back down to the road. They looked around in the road, looking for tracks, stood around for a while talking and panting, then trudged off the north side of the road and made their way down to the river. Soon they had settled down.

Like-a-Pumpkin watched from up on the ridge until he was convinced that they were going to stay, probably for the night. After a little more milling around, all three Chickasaws stretched out on the ground. Like-a-Pumpkin walked down the mountainside to the road, and he walked past the sleeping Chickasaws, headed for home.

Ten

TWO ANI-KUTANI stood outside the door of Standing-in-the-Doorway's private chamber. They stood silently, patiently waiting to be noticed. One was tall and rangy with big bones and a hard, angular face. There were tattoos on his cheeks and throat, on his chest, arms and thighs. He wore earplugs so large that, if he took them out, he could shove all four fingers of one hand into the hole in his lobe. His companion, at least a head shorter, was stocky, and he was similarly decorated. In addition to earplugs, he wore a shiny disc of pounded mica dangling from his nasal septum. Now and then they glanced at one another. Otherwise they did not move.

Standing-in-the-Doorway at last took notice of them.

"What do you want of me?" he said.

The two priests could not see into the unlit room. They only heard the voice coming to them from the darkness.

"We were told to come to see you," said the tall one.

"By Two Heads. I am Ducks Under. This is Lying-in-Wait-Beside-the-Path here with me."

"Come in," said Standing-in-the-Doorway.

The two priests stepped tentatively into the dark chamber. Standing-in-the-Doorway picked a hot coal out of a clay pot in the corner and lit tobacco in the bowl of a short-stemmed clay pipe. The outline of his face glowed red for an instant as the two men waited to hear from him. Clouds of smoke formed around Standing-in-the-Doorway's head as the eyes of the other two slowly became accustomed to the dim light.

"Do you know why you're here?" asked Standing-in-the-Doorway.

"No," said Ducks Under. "We were only told to come here. That's all."

"Yes," said Lying-in-Wait-Beside-the-Path. "By Two Heads."

"I know. I sent him for you. You are warriors?"

"Yes," said Ducks Under. "I've killed Shawnees, Delawares, Chickasaws, Choctaws."

"In fights or from ambush?"

"Both ways."

"And you?" said Standing-in-the-Doorway, turning toward Lying-in-Wait-Beside-the-Path.

"I've fought and killed all enemies of the Real People since I was a boy."

"With what weapons?" said Standing-in-the-Doorway.

"Arrows, warclub, knife, my bare hands."

"And have you ever killed one of the Real People?"

The two warrior-priests looked at one another for an instant, then looked at the floor.

"Would you?" said Standing-in-the-Doorway.

"If one tried to kill me, I would kill him, I suppose," said Ducks Under.

Standing-in-the-Doorway drew deeply on his pipe, and the small room seemed to fill with smoke in hovering layers.

"You know that we are desperate for rain," he said. "And you know that in times like this the welfare of all our people is my responsibility."

"Yes," said Ducks Under.

"We know," said Lying-in-Wait-Beside-the-Path.

"You also know that one person among us can disturb the balance and harmony by doing wrong things or by failing to do that which he should."

The two priests nodded their heads in unison.

"I've done all the things that I should do in normal times," Standing-in-the-Doorway continued. "When it became obvious to me that something was wrong and that methods beyond the ordinary were called for, I sent three priests to the West to find the house of Thunder and to bring back the rain. You know about that?"

"Yes," said Ducks Under. "They were Water Moccasin, Deadwood Lighter and Like-a-Pumpkin."

"They've not returned, and it hasn't rained," said Standing-in-the-Doorway. "And so I conducted the big ceremony, an ancient ceremony long unused. I revived it for the good of all, and I even made the ultimate sacrifice. I slaughtered a daughter of the Real People that we might have rain. And yet it has not rained."

The two priests were getting more nervous. They still did not know why they had been summoned to listen to this narration of recent past events with which they were already familiar.

"What would you do for your people?" said Standing-in-the-Doorway, suddenly turning on the two. "What would you do for me?"

"Anything," said Ducks Under, quickly and defensively. "Anything at all. Anything within my power."

"I, too," said the other.

"None of these things I've done has worked, and I have only just learned why. In Ijodi there is a man called Edohi. Before the ceremony, he was told to supply deer and turkeys. He went out as if to hunt, but he did not come back for the ceremony. His neglect is the reason the ceremony has not worked."

He paused and puffed his pipe and allowed his full message to sink into the brains of the two warrior-priests, and then he spoke again.

"Find Edohi and kill him."

When the two warrior-priests had left, Standing-in-the-Doorway again sat alone in his room. He continued to smoke until the tobacco in his pipe was all burned and the fire was out. Sooner or later, he thought, unless it is indeed the end of the world, sooner or later it will rain. Between now and then, all I have to do is keep the people convinced that the fault does not lie with me. This Edohi can buy me some more time.

Lying-in-Wait-Beside-the-Path was standing just outside the wall of Men's Town. He was beside the entrance waiting for Ducks Under. When they had left Standing-in-the-Doorway's chamber, they had separated to go and arm themselves, having agreed to meet again there where Lying-in-Wait-Beside-the-Path was standing. He had a knife at his waist and a wooden, ball-headed warclub. On his back was a quiver of arrows, and he held a long bow in his right hand.

Ducks Under came out. He was similarly armed, but his warclub had an egg-shaped stone head.

"I'm ready," he said.

"What do you know of this Edohi?" asked Lying-in-Wait-Beside-the-Path.

"Very little," said Ducks Under. "They say he's a great hunter. I also heard that recently he went up into the Shawnee country and captured a slave whom he brought back alive to Ijodi."

"Then he can fight."

"I expect so," said Ducks Under. "When we find him, I think we should both attack him at once and kill him by surprise if we can."

"Yes. I agree."

"Well then," said Ducks Under, "let's go to Ijodi."

Gnat was sitting in his usual spot watching the road to the West. His mother had questioned him that morning when he left the house, and he had given her vague answers. He wished that his uncle, Like-a-Pumpkin, would hurry home, for it was becoming increasingly difficult to watch for him while keeping his purpose a secret. He had already confided his secret to one man, that man Edohi. He wondered if that had been a mistake, but he wasn't too worried about it. He had liked Edohi, and he trusted him.

Still, it might have been better had he kept his secret to himself.

He had stared long and hard, and his eyes were tired, and he had not seen anyone walking down the road that day. He had not seen a cloud in the sky. He knew that when he saw his uncle coming, he would also see the clouds. Or if he should see a cloud in the sky, his uncle would be along soon. He knew that. But so far, he had seen neither. Where was Like-a-Pumpkin? How much longer would it be?

A rabbit jumped out of some tall brown grass off to Gnat's right and sat staring at him, almost in front of him. Gnat expected the rabbit to flee when it saw how close it was to man, but it didn't. It sat there, looking at him, twitching its split nose. Then Gnat had a strong sense that the rabbit was trying to tell him something. It was a foolish thought, but it persisted.

"What, Jisdu?" he said, finally giving in to the thought. "What is it?"

The rabbit turned quickly and sprang back into the tall grass and was gone.

Gone-in-the-Water saw what the women were doing in Ijodi. He was in his house which was outside the walls of the town, yet he saw, and he chuckled.

"I knew it would come," he said. "Didn't I tell you, Ugly? I did, too. Ask Noisy. He knows I told you. I've seen it coming for a long time."

He hobbled across the room and picked up a bowl in which there were pieces of cooked fish. He picked one out and shoved it in his mouth, munching it as he carried the bowl with him back to his bench on the other side of the room. He sat down and picked out another piece. Then he put the bowl on the floor.

"There," he said. "Help yourselves. It's good."

He swallowed, then pushed the second morsel between his wrinkled lips.

"They've been asking for it for a long time," he said. "Acting arrogant. Better than everyone else. Then they made new rules. Laws. Made them up. Telling the men they couldn't go look for their own stolen children. Stolen by Choctaws. And after I had carefully prepared them for war. What? Yes. I had. And they changed the old stories. Some of them. They did that. The young people don't even know the original stories. Young people don't know anything until they've been told, and if they've been told wrong, well, then they just won't know."

He swallowed again, and he reached down to the bowl for another bite.

"And they can't even make it rain. Three priests gone west to look for Thunder. Ha. And the big ceremony. They did it all wrong, you know. I remember it. The way it ought to be done. They didn't ask me. Instead they killed the woman. Young woman. A woman I prepared for marriage. Yes. It was she.

"You didn't eat all of that. Have some more.

"And it hasn't rained, has it? No. It hasn't. But it's coming. I know what the women are up to. For a long time they just grumbled and complained. Grumbling and complaining. That was all. But not now. Then they began to plot. And it's coming. It's coming. Real soon now, it's coming."

Eleven

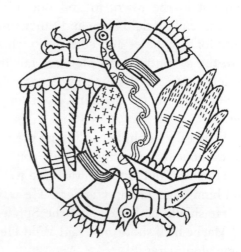

KANASTA had been abandoned for just about a year. The garden plots needed a rest, so the people had cleared themselves new fields, built a new town and simply abandoned the old one. It was about the same size as Ijodi, but it had no wall around it, and since the people had left, it had new inhabitants. Birds nested in the houses, squirrels on the roofs, snakes and lizards ran in and out. Some of the houses were crumbling. In time the forest would reclaim the area, and no one would be able to tell that a town had ever been there. But that would be later. The buildings, for the most part, still stood. And Kanasta was within easy walking distance of Ijodi.

They met by appointment in the abandoned townhouse of Kanasta. Most of the people from Ijodi were there, and there were people from other towns as well. There were men and women, old and young. And there were children. Some sat in the townhouse with their parents, others ran wild out in the town, in and out of the mostly empty houses, sending field mice and other small creatures scurrying for new holes and corners in which to hide.

In the townhouse, people were talking in small groups while waiting for the meeting to actually get under way. Wild Hemp and the Spoiler were talking with Hemp Carrier.

"Why isn't Edohi here?" asked the Spoiler. "Didn't he know about the meeting? Didn't you tell him?"

"He knew, but when it was time to come, we couldn't find him," said Hemp Carrier. "He wasn't in town."

"He should be here," said the Spoiler.

"Maybe he'll show up," said Wild Hemp. "Maybe he'll come along later."

"Well," said the Spoiler, "we should start." She turned to Hemp Carrier. "You should speak to them," she said. "You're his uncle."

Hemp Carrier stepped out into the center of the room, and in a moment the room was quiet. Solemnly, Hemp Carrier surveyed the crowd. The sounds of children playing outside could be heard in the silence of the big room. Hemp Carrier took a deep breath.

"Brothers and sisters," he said, "we are here to make important decisions. For as long as any of us here can remember, the *Ani-Kutani* have been at Men's Town. Our fathers and our fathers' fathers and their fathers before them knew the *Ani-Kutani*. They have always kept the ancient secrets, told and interpreted for us the ancient tales. They have kept our ceremonies, the ceremonies that bring the rain and make the crops grow. We have always believed that the things they do and the things they tell us to do and not to do keep us walking in balance here between the other two worlds.

"We know all these things, and we have considered all these things. Had it not been for the importance of all this to our lives and to the lives of all our children, some of us would surely have acted sooner. For the *Ani-Kutani* have gone far beyond their rightful authority. They have gone from working for our benefit to ruling over us. The Real People were never meant to be ruled over by anyone."

Hemp Carrier then outlined again all of the complaints regarding the *Ani-Kutani*. He spoke of their general overbearing attitude, their gradual assumption of power and finally their specific recent abuses of power culminating in the startling ritual sacrifice of Corn Flower. Finally he argued that no matter what the priests had done, should or should not have done, their supposed powers were not what they were supposed to be, for if they were, it would have rained.

It was quiet for a space when Hemp Carrier stopped talking. Then someone in the crowd spoke up.

"The priests are saying that it's Edohi's fault that it hasn't rained. Edohi didn't do his part at the ceremony."

The Spoiler jumped up in anger.

"He gave a wife," she shouted. "My daughter. What more would you have him give?"

Hemp Carrier looked at the Spoiler and held a hand up, asking her to be quiet and be patient. She sat back down, a scowl on her face.

"Everyone has a right to speak here," said Hemp Carrier. "We want all questions to be answered. We want everyone to be agreed. I know of the latest claim made by the priests, but I don't believe it. It's another excuse for their own failure. They told us the three priests would bring the rain from Thunder's house. When they failed, they said the big ceremony would do it. That failed. They said we had to wait for seven days. The seven days passed. Then they said it was Edohi's fault. What will they say next?"

"It should have been a virgin," said old Gone-in-the-Water. He was sitting close to the door by himself, leaning against the wall. His voice was low and weak, barely audible. He was puffing on his pipe.

"What did you say?" asked Hemp Carrier.

"In the old ceremony it was a virgin who was killed. They didn't even do the ceremony the right way. It should have been a virgin."

Two Heads had gone to Ijodi to spread the word that Edohi was to blame for the failure of the ceremony. He had sent other priests to other towns on the same mission, but he had thought that he himself might be more effective in his own home town. He was puzzled, though, to find Ijodi almost deserted. He hurried to his mother's house and was a little relieved when he found her at home.

"Mother," he said, "where is everyone?"

"I don't know," she said. "They don't tell me anymore what they're doing or where they're going. I think it's because of you."

"What do you mean?"

"They think that if I know anything, I might tell you.

They don't want you to know. They don't want it to get back to Men's Town."

"Are they plotting against us then?" asked Two Heads. "Against the *Ani-Kutani?*"

"Yes. I think so. I think that's what they're doing, and that's what most of my friends think, too. The friends that I have left."

"Where are they now? Where did they go?"

"I don't know. They left. That's all. Maybe they're moving away to start a new town somewhere. I don't know."

Two Heads rushed out of his mother's house. He looked around frantically but saw no one. He started toward the gateway to leave the town when two women stepped out of a house to intercept him. He stopped.

"We're not with them," said one of the women. "With those others. We're loyal to the *Ani-Kutani.*"

"You're not with whom?" asked Two Heads.

"The others. All of them. Well, most of them."

"The main one is the Spoiler," said the other woman. "She's the leader. She's mad because of her daughter."

"And Wild Hemp and her brother Hemp Carrier. Them, too."

"But almost everyone has joined with them."

"Joined with them for what?" said Two Heads. "What are they doing?"

"They're plotting. That's what. We knew it when they stopped talking to us and stopped complaining out loud. They started whispering and meeting together secretly. Well, we knew they were meeting, but they kept it secret what they were saying."

"We knew, though, that they were plotting against you, against the priests."

"Just what are they planning?" said Two Heads.

"We don't know," said one of the women. "They won't talk to us anymore."

"Where have they gone?"

"I don't know for sure, but they were walking toward Kanasta when they left here. There's nothing else that way. Just Kanasta."

"But no one lives there anymore," said Two Heads.

"That's where they went, I think."

"What better place for a secret meeting?" said the other.

Two Heads turned and raced away from the women. He left the town, hesitated for a moment, then headed for Kanasta. He considered going back to Men's Town to tell Standing-in-the-Doorway what he had learned, but he wasn't quite sure just what he had learned, and Kanasta was closer to Ijodi than was Men's Town and in the opposite direction. If he took the time to go to Men's Town, maybe no one would be able to get to Kanasta before the meeting was over. Someone should catch them at the meeting, he thought. Someone should find out just exactly what they were up to over there. He was a little afraid to go to Kanasta alone, but he was even more afraid, he realized, for the ultimate safety of Standing-in-the-Doorway and the security of the *Ani-Kutani*. Besides, he thought, what could the people do? They would be the ones who would be afraid when they realized that they had been caught conspiring by a *Kutani*. What would he do when he caught them? He didn't know. He only knew that he felt an urgency to get there and to find out what was going on.

Edohi sat alone on the mountaintop just outside of Ijodi. He had watched the people leaving town to go to the secret meeting at Kanasta. His uncle had told him about the meeting, and Edohi felt a little guilty that he was deliberately avoiding it. He should be with them, he knew. Why then was he not? He was not afraid to fight, not even to die. It was something else, something he did not understand about himself. But he wanted to be alone. He did not want to be a part of a crowd, much less part of a group conspiracy. And he had no will for action. He had not confided in his uncle, Hemp Carrier, about these feelings. Instead he had simply left town and climbed the mountain and stayed.

"We are all agreed then that all the priests must die?" said Hemp Carrier. He waited a sufficient period of time for any response, and there was no dissent. "Then it shall be so," he concluded.

"How do we proceed from here?" said Big Bear.

"We should select a leader for the fight," said Hemp Carrier. "The leader will decide then just how to proceed."

"Who will it be?" someone asked.

All eyes were on Hemp Carrier. He knew that in a moment someone would name him, and then, more than likely, the rest would give their assent. Hemp Carrier had experience in war. He had won many honors. And he had been among the most vocal in calling for this revolt against the priests. It was logical, and, of course, he would willingly accept the responsibility should it happen that way. But Hemp Carrier did not want it to happen that way. He considered the battle being planned to be one of great importance. It would not be like a fight between the Real People and Choctaws or Senecas or Catawbas. It would be Real People killing Real People, a thing under ordinary circumstances to be avoided at all costs, and it seemed to Hemp Carrier that the selection of a leader for this fight required a different approach. Before anyone could shout out his name, he held up his arms for silence, and he walked across the room to stand before Gone-in-the-Water.

"Uncle," he said respectfully, "can you tell us who should be the leader in this fight?"

"Of course," said Gone-in-the-Water. "It's Edohi."

Twelve

TWO HEADS hurried toward Kanasta. The road was barely a path, having gone largely unused for almost a year. It occurred to Two Heads that a good rain would probably allow the growth of the forest to completely overwhelm the path in a very short time indeed. He felt nervous and agitated, and he wondered just what was going on with the people of Ijodi, people he had known all of his life, his own family, his friends. What were they so upset about anyway? The drought? Standing-in-the-Doorway was doing everything he could to bring the rain, and it was wrong of the people to blame him. He was a great man. The greatest man on earth. He was the head of the *Ani-Kutani*.

Were they angry over the sacrifice? That seemed likely, as the women in Ijodi had said that the Spoiler was the leading agitator, the one making the most noise and urging the others on. But the sacrifice was simply part of the ceremony, and the ceremony was ancient and honorable and sacred and had been performed for the good of all the people. Of course, he knew in his own mind that Standing-in-the-Doorway had allowed him to select the honored one, and he had selected her out of spite and for personal revenge. But no one else knew that. They could not know it.

He was anxious to get to Kanasta and catch these people at their plotting. He would put the fear of the *Ani-Kutani* in their hearts. He would berate them and threaten them. He would have them begging him to give them another chance, and he could not decide whether or not he would do so. He would certainly make them suffer with worry for a while. He himself had become a very important person. It was, of course, unofficial, but Two Heads was practically the number-two man at Men's Town. No one was as close to Standing-in-the-Doorway as was he. He imagined the fear and astonishment on the faces of the people from Ijodi when he surprised them. It was a wonderful opportunity, he told himself, to put them in their place and at the same time show them what an important man he had become.

Back at Kanasta, the protests had started almost immediately following the startling announcement made by the old conjurer. It couldn't be Edohi, they said. He didn't even care about what was going on. If he did, why wasn't he present? Where was he anyhow? He couldn't be depended on. No one ever even knew where to find him. He stayed too much to himself. Besides, what had he ever done? He had captured the Outcast, but that was all. He was no leader. He was not even one of the pack. He was a loner. When the voices at last quieted down, and everyone had said what he wanted to say, Gone-in-the-Water spoke again, still calm, still quiet.

"Do what you want to do," he said. "It will make no difference. I've already been told. It's Edohi."

"Then we'll just have to find Edohi and tell him," said Hemp Carrier. He looked the crowd over carefully, pausing to determine whether or not there was more dissent. No one spoke. Then Two Heads stalked into the room. He stopped and stood, legs widespread, arms across his chest, and he gave the crowd his sternest look. Hemp Carrier still stood before the crowd, and Two Heads turned toward him.

"What's going on here?" he demanded.

Hemp Carrier's mouth twisted into a half-smile.

"We're looking over this old town," he said. "We might all move here. Ijodi's getting crowded with too many people."

"I want to know what it is you're doing here," Two Heads said.

Picking up a pole from the floor, the Spoiler stood up. The pole was about as long as her leg and was tapered to a point on one end. She pointed the stick menacingly at Two Heads.

"The proper question is this," she said. "What are you doing here? You were not invited, and you're not wanted."

"I stand here a *Kutani*," said Two Heads. "I represent Standing-in-the-Doorway. I can go anyplace I want to go, and I demand to know the reason for this secret gathering."

Hemp Carrier stepped in front of Two Heads and deliberately looked him in the eyes, staring hard. Two Heads had to look away.

"There must be something about the Real People that I don't know," said Hemp Carrier. "Has something happened that I didn't hear about? I have always thought that Real People could go freely wherever they want to go. I have always believed that Real People could gather together anytime and talk about anything they like. Is that no longer true? Can you explain that to me, priestling?"

"It's been reported that you're here to plot against the *Ani-Kutani*," said Two Heads. "That is not allowed. You cannot do that."

The Spoiler moved toward Two Heads shaking her stick.

"You priests are the ones who are doing things you have no right to do," she said. "Giving orders. Taking my daughter. My daughter."

"Everything the *Ani-Kutani* do is done for good reason," Two Heads said. "For the good of all. I had every right to select your daughter for the sacrifice. I had—"

He stopped, frightened. He realized he had said something he should not have said. He suddenly felt, not in charge, but in imminent danger. He had thought that these people would cower before the authority of Men's Town, but they were not cowering. And they were angry. He backed away from the Spoiler.

"I'm leaving," he said. "I'm going back to Men's Town. Standing-in-the-Doorway will hear about this."

Hemp Carrier took hold of Two Heads's right arm, and Two Heads tried to pull himself free. Big Bear jumped up and came at him, reaching out to help Hemp Carrier hold him. He missed and tore loose the priest's robe, leaving Two Heads naked except for breechclout and moccasins. He dropped the robe and grabbed Two Heads's other arm. The young priest struggled, but the two men held him fast.

"Let me go," shouted Two Heads. "How dare you lay hands on me. Standing-in-the-Doorway will kill you all. Let me go."

The Spoiler stepped up close and looked into Two Heads's eyes.

"You," she said. "You selected her. Her playmate. Her childhood friend. Lifelong friend. You're to blame for her death. Why?"

Two Heads's lips quivered and twisted into a snarl, and he returned the Spoiler's stare. His fear seemed to leave him, and he became defiant.

"I hated her," he said. "I've always hated her. She made a fool of me, over and over again. She thought she was better than me, and I hated her, and so I selected her for the sacrifice, and now she's dead."

The Spoiler raised the pointed end of the stick she carried and touched it to the skin just below Two Heads's sternum. She pushed slowly. He looked down, not believing what was happening. The pole was dirty, jagged and splintered. It looked like it was starting to rot. His flesh was puckered around the tip where the Spoiler was pushing it against him. The fear returned. It became panic. He screamed.

"Let me go. Don't."

The Spoiler shoved hard but not deep, breaking skin, pushing the pole perhaps a finger-length deep. She stopped, still looking into his frightened and unbelieving eyes. He shrieked in terror and pain as his blood gushed out hot and sticky. He felt his heart pounding, pumping the blood down to the fresh hole and out. Then the Spoiler rammed the pole forward with all her strength, driving it all the way through his body. Still she held it. Still she stared into his eyes. His shrieking ceased, and his eyes began to glaze.

He remembered vividly the blood of Corn Flower, and he recalled the time he had accosted her, only to have her throw him into the river. He felt again the humiliation. He even thought about the time she had saved him from the Choctaws and about the squirrel she had killed when they were children. Then she had given it to him because he was pouting. He saw her face. He saw her long legs as she ran through the woods. Then deep, dark red slowly flooded his vision, and then everything was black. His head fell forward. His body went limp. The Spoiler released her grip on the pole, and the two men dropped the arms. The body crumpled into a lifeless, pathetic heap in a widening pool of blood that on the dirt floor of the abandoned townhouse looked black, not red. Hemp Carrier looked out over the crowd of fascinated spectators.

"It's begun," he said.

Thirteen

GONE-IN-THE-WATER hurried into his house carrying a short stick. One end of the stick was covered with a small glop of mud. He held out the stick carefully in his right hand as he picked up a small bundle from a corner of the room.

"What? What did you say, Noisy?"

He unwrapped the bundle, a small piece of groundhog skin, to reveal a collection of hairs and nail parings.

"It's my collection. That's all. It's complete now. What? What's on the end of the stick? His spit. What else? Don't you know anything? I was watching him and he spat on the ground. I never thought he would be that careless. The great man. Ha. Yes. Everything else is still here. I have to check it. I never know where things might be with you two around here. Huh? Of course it's all from Men's Town. Where else? I got it. I collected it all.

"Of course they wouldn't let me in to get these things. I

was invisible. How else did you think I would be able to get in and out and gather up hair and nails? What do you mean? You don't believe me? You doubt me? Do you see me all of the time? Well, how do you know, when you don't see me, whether I'm gone someplace or I'm here and invisible? Tell me that. How do you know? You little shit. Go find Ugly and go somewhere with him to get into your mischief. Go on and leave me alone. I have important work to do here."

The old man refolded the skin. He was still holding the stick carefully so the spittle on its end wouldn't touch anything. He looked around the room.

"Now where did I leave my digging stick?" he said. "I thought I left it right over there. I— Noisy. Ugly. Are you here? Ah, there you are. What have you done with my digging stick? This is no time for your pranks. Do you want to help or not? I told you this is important. I'm not just fooling around here."

He held the stick out in front of himself, showing it.

"This is his. Do you understand? What? Whose?"

The conjurer crouched down low and lowered his voice to a whisper.

"Standing-in-the-Doorway himself, that's who. You'd know if you paid attention instead of playing tricks. Now do you understand? What? Oh. Oh, thank you."

He walked to a corner and reached behind a large basket to retrieve the digging stick. He shoved it into the sash he wore tied around his waist, picked up the groundhog skin bundle and headed for the door.

"Well, Little People," he said over his shoulder, "are you coming with me or not?"

. . . .

The Outcast sat off to the side of the Spoiler's house. Big Bear and Wild Hemp were there listening to the Spoiler talk to Hemp Carrier.

"We can't afford much delay," said the Spoiler. "Someone from Men's Town is bound to find out about Two Heads before much longer."

"I'll go right now and look for Edohi," said Hemp Carrier. "I agree with you. He has to be found soon."

"Where will you look for him?" said Wild Hemp.

"I don't know. I'll just go out and start to look around, I guess."

"Several of us should go," said Big Bear. "We can go in different directions."

"I think I may know where to look," said the Outcast.

The others stopped talking and turned to face the Shawnee.

"Where?" said Hemp Carrier.

"The mountaintop just outside of the entrance to this town, there beside the road," said the Outcast. "There's a place up there where there are large, flat boulders. You can sit on them and overlook the whole town and a long stretch of the road. Edohi goes there sometimes."

"I know the place," said Hemp Carrier. "I'll go there right now. Wait for me to get back before you or any others go out. I won't be gone long."

They watched Hemp Carrier leave, and soon after, Wild Hemp and Big Bear took their leave. The Spoiler stood in front of her house. The Outcast was in his usual place off to the side. She looked in his direction.

"Come on," she said. "Come and eat with me."

The Outcast felt his heart leap. It was the first time she had spoken kindly to him. She had hated him up until he had saved her daughter Sohi from the rattlesnake. Then she had given him his freedom, not reluctantly, but perfunctorily. She had freed him as if she had been paying a debt, nothing more. And since then he had stayed close to her, waiting for a chance to be of help, hoping for a word of encouragement, but she had merely tolerated his presence. At last the kind word had come. He walked over to stand beside her.

Gone-in-the-Water picked his way through the woods, looking carefully before taking each step. There was deadfall in the woods and beneath it uneven ground and hidden outcroppings of rock. He was old, and his bones, he knew, were brittle. He was no longer surefooted as he had been in his youth. One stumble, one unlucky fall, and he could lie there on the forest floor with broken bones and slowly die a lonely and a painful death. No one would know what had happened. No one would know where he had gone. In a few days someone would surely come looking for him at his house for medicine or for advice. Eventually they would know that he was missing, and they would probably go out looking for him. But it was likely, he thought, that in such a case, someone at some time in the distant future would simply chance upon his bones. He had to be especially careful walking through the woods alone. Well, almost alone.

"Ugly," he said, "what would you do if I were to fall and break my leg here in the woods? Would you show yourself to someone else and tell him where to find me?

Would you, Noisy? Or would you leave me here to starve and rot? You'd play with my bones, wouldn't you? I know your evil little minds."

He stepped carefully over a large fallen branch, and a green lizard scurried away to find a hiding place. Breathing heavily, the old man sat down on the branch.

"Well," he said, "I'm not so young anymore. I have to rest awhile. Just a little. Don't be so impatient with me. I just want to catch my breath. That's all. It won't take long."

He drew in long, deep breaths, trying to steady his breathing and calm his body back down. He raised his head and looked around.

"You know," he said, "this might be a good enough place right here. What? Why not? Right over there at the base of that ash. No one would find it there. Oh, you think you know everything, you two. Well, all right then. You lead the way. You tell me where if you're so smart. Yes. Yes. I'm ready to go now. Go ahead. I'll be right behind you."

He stood up slowly and started walking again. In a short while the ground beneath his feet began to slope downward, not sharply, gradually, but enough to make him slow his pace even more. When he reached the bottom of the slope, he found himself standing in a dry creek bed.

"Here?" he said. "Right here? Well, all right then. Move over out of the way."

He squatted, and he placed the groundhog skin bundle carefully on the ground to one side. The saliva-tipped stick he still held up in one hand. With his free hand he pulled the digging stick loose from the sash around his waist, and he began jabbing it into the ground, tossing the loose dirt aside. Now and then he stopped poking at the earth in order to catch his breath. When the hole was long enough and deep enough to suit his purpose, he laid aside the digging stick, then placed the spit-stick in the hole.

"Ah," he said. "There it is."

He picked up the bundle of hair and nail parings and set it in the hole with the stick. Then with his bare hands, he raked the dirt back into the hole. He patted the dirt down and carelessly scattered leaves over all to hide the evidence of what he had just done.

"Yes," he said. "You were right. That's just fine."

He shifted his weight in order to drop onto his knees, and looking down at the ground there where he had buried his strange collection, he began to quietly intone a brief charm.

> You *Ani-Kutani*,
> I've just put you under the ground.
> They, not you, will be successful.
> Your souls will be wandering
> aimlessly there in the Ghost Country.
> They will never rest.

He stood up slowly and with some difficulty, his old legs tingling from their recent temporarily impaired circulation.

"Ah," he said. "I'm too old. What? Oh."

He took a few steps and bent over to pick up from the

ground a long, stout pole, just right for him to use as a staff.

"Thank you, Noisy," he said. "Where's Ugly?"

He looked around some more.

"Oh, there you are. Well, I'm all done here. Let's go home," he said.

Fourteen

EDOHI SAT on the mountaintop alone. He had lost track of how many days he had spent thus, but he didn't really care. He felt as if, at his young age, the best part of his life was over. He had enjoyed such a brief period of married life. It was like a cruel joke. He had been given such joy, it seemed, only so he would know what he was missing when it was then taken away. He could imagine no further pleasure in life. He had no interest in other women. War honors held no excitement for him. He did not want to live longer in Ijodi under the shadow of Men's Town, yet he couldn't think of any other place he would want to live either. So he sat alone on the mountaintop, day after day, doing nothing at all.

He was sitting on the ground on the downhill side of the flat rocks leaning back against them when he heard the footsteps approaching from behind him. It must be the Outcast, he thought, coming again to try to talk to him, to try again to convince him that he should resume his life. He wished that he had scooted farther down when he sat, so that he would be well hidden. Then maybe the Shawnee would go away. But it was too late for that. He knew that at least the top of his head was showing above the rock from back there. Well, he would not talk. He had nothing to say. After a while, the man would give up in frustration and leave him alone in peace. Then he heard the voice, and it was not the voice of the Outcast.

"Is that you, Edohi, there behind the rock?"

"Who are you?" said Edohi.

"I'm called Ducks Under, and this is Lying-in-Wait-Beside-the-Path here with me."

Edohi turned. On his knees, he looked over the rock at the two armed men standing there.

"You're from Men's Town," he said. "You're *Ani-Kutani.*"

"And you are Edohi," said Ducks Under.

"Yes. What do you want with me?"

"We've come to kill you, Edohi," said Ducks Under. "We were sent by Standing-in-the-Doorway himself."

"And why does the great man take such a personal and special interest in me?" Edohi asked. The sarcastic tone of his voice was not wasted on the two warrior-priests.

"You didn't do your part for the ceremony," said Lying-in-Wait-Beside-the-Path. "Because of that the ceremony didn't work. And because of that, you have to die."

"Put aside your bows," said Edohi, "and I'll come out from behind this rock and fight with you. I'm not afraid to die. I don't care if you kill me, but I don't want to be killed like a deer."

The two *Ani-Kutani* looked at one another and shrugged. They tossed their bows off to the side, pulled the quivers of arrows off their backs and tossed them after the bows. They pulled their warclubs loose from their waists and waited. Ducks Under grinned. The other scowled. Edohi stood up and walked slowly around the boulder.

"You're not even armed," said Ducks Under.

"I don't need weapons to fight priests," Edohi sneered.

Ducks Under slipped his warclub back into the band around his waist.

"You take him," he said to his companion, and he moved to one side, crossing his arms over his chest.

"You don't need weapons to die," said Lying-in-Wait. He moved toward Edohi, and Edohi started to move toward his own left, circling the priest, making it awkward for him to swing his warclub in his right hand. The *Kutani* turned trying to keep Edohi in front of him. Growing impatient, he stepped forward and took a wild swing. Edohi sidestepped it easily.

"You'll have to come closer than that," he said, and he continued circling, moving faster. Lying-in-Wait roared his anger and frustration and rushed at Edohi, warclub held high over his head. Edohi ducked low and stepped forward, hitting the *Kutani*'s knees. The man fell across Edohi's back and landed on his face on the hard, rocky ground. Edohi stepped back and waited for his opponent to stand. Lying-in-Wait turned quickly to his back. He glared at Edohi. His face was scratched from his fall. He stood up slowly and deliberately, still firmly gripping the ball-headed warclub in his right hand.

He lunged forward, taking a wide sideways swipe at Edohi from right to left. Edohi jumped back to avoid the blow, then, while the other was still half turned from his wild swing, he stepped forward and kicked hard and high, clouting Lying-in-Wait across the right side of his back. Lying-in-Wait staggered, nearly falling. Edohi couldn't be sure, but he thought that he might have cracked a couple of the man's ribs. He moved quickly, reaching around Lying-in-Wait's body from behind, pinning his arms to his sides. He grasped his own wrist and squeezed. Lying-in-Wait howled in pain, and Edohi knew then that his kick had indeed broken ribs.

"Ducks Under," said Lying-in-Wait, "kill him. I'm hurt. Kill him."

Ducks Under pulled loose his own warclub once more, and he walked toward the fight. He was within three paces when Edohi shoved Lying-in-Wait forward, and the two warrior-priests collided with each other and fell to the ground. Lying-in-Wait yelped his pain again as he fell on top of Ducks Under. Edohi backed away a few steps.

"So it will take two priests after all to kill one unarmed man," he said.

Ducks Under pushed Lying-in-Wait off to one side and got to his feet. He reached down to the ground to pick up the warclub Lying-in-Wait had dropped. Flipping it in the air, he caught it by its ball head. Then he took a step toward Edohi offering him the handle.

"Take it," he said. "I'll still kill you."

Edohi hesitated a moment, then reached out and gripped the handle. He stepped back again quickly.

"Now," said Ducks Under, and he swung his club at

Edohi's head. Edohi blocked the blow with the other club. With the two weapons still locked together overhead, Ducks Under grabbed Edohi's throat with his left hand. Edohi shoved his own left hand into the face of Ducks Under, and his fingers groped for eyes.

"Kill him," shouted Lying-in-Wait.

Then with a sudden wrenching, the combatants separated. Crouched for attack, they circled each other. And Edohi, whose moves had all thus far been defensive, rushed into the taller, lanky Ducks Under. He crashed into Ducks Under's midsection with his shoulder, and the force of the impact bore the larger man to the ground on his back. Both men lost their warclubs. Edohi straddled the chest of Ducks Under, kneeling on his arms, and he clutched the *Kutani*'s throat with both hands and began to squeeze.

Ducks Under's eyes opened wide. His mouth struggled to suck air into his lungs but to no avail. He kicked and flailed with his legs, but Edohi held him fast and squeezed harder and harder. Ducks Under's face turned a deep, dark purple, and Lying-in-Wait, realizing what was happening, ran for the nearest warclub. He winced in pain from the broken ribs as he bent to pick up the weapon and again as he raised it high in preparation for dealing the death blow. But he stopped, warclub poised on high, astonishment on his face, as a bloody, flint-tipped arrow emerged from his chest. He realized with horror that it had been shot from behind him, that it had been driven all the way through from his back. It was his last thought. He fell forward dead. Edohi continued squeezing the other's throat until he was sure he had choked the life out of the man. He released his deadly grip slowly and turned to see who it was that had come to his aid.

"Uncle," he said, surprised.

"I came looking for you, nephew," said Hemp Carrier, "it seems just in time."

"Yes," said Edohi. "I suppose."

He stood up, stepping over the body there beneath him, and he turned away from his uncle, breathing deeply, pacing nervously.

"What do you mean?" said Hemp Carrier. "If I hadn't come when I did, the man would almost certainly have killed you."

"Yes. Probably. But, Uncle, I have no reason to live. I don't even know why I fought these men, except that in here with all of my other feelings, there is yet a rage. They came here deliberately to kill me, you know. They said that Standing-in-the-Doorway himself had sent them. I spoiled the ceremony, they said. So you see, it doesn't matter about me. Since these two failed, they'll only send more.

"But they had no reason to want you dead—until now. You killed one of them. Now they will want to kill you, and so will this man's kin. You shouldn't have come here, and you shouldn't have killed this man."

"Edohi," said Hemp Carrier, "there are things you don't know. Things that have just happened. That's why I came here. To tell you. Sit down now and listen to me."

Edohi paced around a little more. Then he walked to the rock and sat. Hemp Carrier followed and sat beside him.

"We went to Kanasta," he said.

"Yes," said Edohi. "I know. I didn't go because— I didn't go. I don't know why."

"It doesn't matter. We had the meeting. Most of the people from Ijodi were there, and there were people from other towns as well. All of the seven clans were represented, and at last everyone agreed."

He paused, and he stared at the two bodies lying not far away. Flies were greedily attacking them already.

"Agreed to what?" asked Edohi.

"The priests have gone too far," said Hemp Carrier. "They must all be killed."

"They all agreed to that?"

"Yes. All who were there. There are a few people who remain loyal to the *Ani-Kutani*, but they weren't invited. The people agreed that they won't be harmed as long as they stay home. Just stay out of the way. We also agreed that no clan will hold anyone responsible for the killing of any *Kutani*, no matter what his clan."

Edohi seemed stunned by this news. He stood up and walked away from his uncle a few steps, and when he spoke, it was with his back still turned on Hemp Carrier.

"I never thought to see this happen," he said. He turned to face his uncle once again. "They will really try to kill all the priests?"

"We will kill all the priests, Edohi. We. They and I and you. It's already started. We've just killed these two right here. And at Kanasta, the Spoiler killed Two Heads. It started already. Now we have to finish it. There's no turning back."

"Two Heads is dead? Acorn?"

"Yes."

"The Spoiler killed him?"

"He was the one who selected the victim for the sacrifice."

"Two Heads?"

"Yes."

Edohi lifted his head toward the Sky Vault and roared his anguished outrage. Hemp Carrier waited patiently until Edohi was again quiet.

"You, Edohi," he said, "have been chosen to lead the fight."

Fifteen

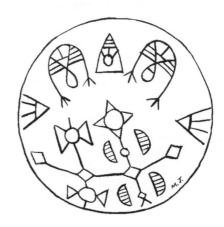

THEY MET on the mountaintop, Edohi and Hemp Carrier and two men from each clan:

Ani-Waya, the Wolf Clan, was represented by Big Foot and Trotting Wolf.

Stinging Ant and Agili were there for *Ani-Kawi*, the Deer Clan.

Ani-Tsisqua, the Bird Clan, Edohi's own clan, had sent Rock Thrower and Beavertail.

From *Ani-Sakonige*, the Blue People, Fog-Rolling-In and Allbones had come.

Pot-Kicker and Burntwood were Paint People, *Ani-Wodi*.

Ani-Gatagewi, Wild Potato People, sent Big Bear, Edohi's father, and Crawfish.

And the Long Hairs, *Ani-Gilohi*, had chosen Bullfrog and Bear Meat to represent them.

These fourteen men would hear Edohi's plan and take

word back to their own people. Edohi stood before them, and Hemp Carrier stood off to the side. The bodies of the two dead priests still lay where they had fallen. By the time everyone had gathered, there wasn't much of the day left, and there would be much to be done by the morning. Edohi stepped up on the big boulder.

"Brothers," he said, "you know that I did not seek this role. It was thrust upon me. But I embrace it, and we will succeed, or I will die in the attempt.

"We have all been wronged by the *Ani-Kutani*. Our course is clear, and our cause is just. All seven clans have sent their sons to Men's Town to become priests, and all seven clans have agreed that there will be no revenge for any dead priests. We all renounce them. They are *Ani-Kutani* and nothing more, and therefore they are now our enemies. All must die.

"And this thing we are about to do must be done quickly. It must be done at once. There can be no delay, no long fight.

"When we leave here tonight, spread the word among all your people. Inside the walls of Men's Town are one hundred and fifty priests. They're not all warrior-priests, but all can fight. And all will fight when we attack. We must raise two hundred at least. So meet me before the Sun comes out in the morning. Everyone who wants to fight. Bring all of your weapons: bows and arrows, war-clubs, knives, blowguns and darts, whatever you have.

"Wolf People, bring fire.

"We will utterly destroy the *Ani-Kutani*."

The fourteen men started down the mountainside to

put into motion Edohi's plan. Edohi and Hemp Carrier were left alone.

"Uncle," said Edohi, "what we are about to do, could it mean the end of the world?"

"The *Ani-Kutani* would have us think so," said Hemp Carrier, "but I don't believe it."

"But the ceremonies keep our world in balance. If it becomes unbalanced, chaos will follow. The *uk'ten'*, Tlanuwa the giant hawk, all of the creatures from the Underworld will be among us again."

"Are you afraid?"

"I'm not afraid of the priests. I do fear what might follow. If we kill them."

"But you already told the people that you'd meet them in the morning to lead the attack on Men's Town."

"And I will. Since I've been chosen, I'll do it. But I am afraid of the future."

"Edohi," said Hemp Carrier, "go see Gone-in-the-Water. Tell him your fears. See what he has to tell you. I think he'll put your mind at ease."

"All right. I'll go to see him now."

Edohi headed for his path down the mountainside. About to descend, he stopped and turned to face Hemp Carrier again.

"Uncle," he said. "I want something done before morning."

"What is it?"

"I want someone to go to Kanasta and someone to come up here. I want the bodies of the three dead priests brought to Men's Town in the morning."

. . . .

Gone-in-the-Water was behind his house. The Sun was low in the West, and the light was dim, but the old man knew just where he was going. At the base of a large, old oak, he shoved his leathery old hand into a hold underneath one of the large roots. It came out clutching a folded deerskin. He took the small bundle and went back to his house. Inside, he knelt on the floor, his old knees popping and cracking as they bent, and he put the bundle on the floor. Fumbling for a while with the knot, he at last untied the short piece of rawhide strip which held the bundle together. He unfolded the deerskin to reveal a shining crystal the size of a duck's egg. Gingerly, he picked it up between his thumb and his index finger and held it up in front of his face, gazing intently into it. He spoke to it in harsh whispered tones, and he turned it this way and that, catching in its facets the fading evening light that came in streaks through his door and through the cracks in his walls. Then he held it still and stared. He watched, fascinated, as an image appeared in the bottom of the crystal just above where his thumb held it and slowly rose to the top before it vanished.

He wrapped the crystal back up and retied the bundle. He stood up, his joints creaking their complaints, and went back outside. Looking around to make sure that no one was watching, he walked back into the woods to locate a new hiding place for the crystal.

He had been back in his house just long enough to catch his breath when Edohi came.

"Come in," he said. "Sit down. I've been expecting you."

Edohi was not surprised by that announcement. All his life long, he had heard of the incredible powers of Gone-in-the-Water, and it was widely believed that the old man always knew when someone was coming to visit him. He even knew who was coming and what the person wanted, it was said. Edohi ducked to get through the low doorway and sat on the bench against the back wall.

"I don't have any *gah-no-hey-nuh* to offer you," said the conjurer. "I'm a bad host since my wife went away to the Ghost Country. That was when you were only this high."

He held his hand up about level with his waist.

"I know, Uncle," said Edohi, using the common respectful form of address for elders. "Uncle, they have decided to kill all of the *Ani-Kutani.*"

"Yes," said Gone-in-the-Water. "I know."

"They have made me the leader in this fight."

"Yes. I know." The old man smiled a sly smile.

"Uncle, I'm not afraid to fight. I'm not afraid to die, but I am afraid of disturbing the balance. I don't know if it's right, this thing we're about to do. I don't know what terrible things might happen to this world if we kill all the priests."

Gone-in-the-Water went to a corner of his room for his pipe and tobacco. He filled the pipe bowl, then located the clay pot in which he kept hot coals. He plucked out one small, red-hot ember and dropped it in on the tobacco while sucking deeply on the stem to get the pipe going. The small room was almost immediately filled with heavy smoke. The old man went back to the bench and sat down again beside Edohi. He offered the pipe to his visitor. Edohi took it and puffed, then handed it back.

"It's true," said Gone-in-the-Water, "as far as I know, that there are three worlds. There's the world on top of the Sky Vault where Thunder lives, and Selu the Corn Mother, and the Ghost Country is there. That's where all our souls will go one day. It's also where we came from originally. I mean, our first ancestors came from there. All the life forms we know on this world existed first up there, and the original of each is still there. But it got crowded, so some of them came down here to live. In those days, though, there was nothing here but water.

"When the first animals came down from the Sky Vault, they found they couldn't stand or sit on the water. Oh, you know the story. At last the water beetle dove down deep and brought up mud and spread it out on top, and the buzzard dried it with his wings. So there was the world on top and this world, but there's another world beneath this one.

"And in that Underworld down there below us, everything is opposite the way it is here. When we have day, they have night. When we have winter, they have summer. Down there are all the giants, the water cannibals, who sometimes come up here through the waterways, all the frightening creatures from the early days of the world.

"And this world on which we walk between the other two is indeed in a delicate situation. The other two worlds are full of powerful spirits, and their forces are opposed to each other. If we lose our balance, we will be crushed, torn apart, when the two opposites meet and mix. We would have no defense.

"So we do things in certain ways. We have our ceremonies and our rituals and other things we do and don't do.

All that is calculated to help us maintain our balance on this middle world. Yes, nephew, I know your fears."

He took a puff on his pipe and handed it to Edohi, and Edohi smoked.

"Well," said the conjurer, "the *Ani-Kutani* have had charge of our ceremonies. They have led us to believe that they are the ones who keep the balance for us. They have created your fears, Edohi."

Edohi handed the pipe to Gone-in-the-Water.

"I don't understand, Uncle," he said.

"Do you spit in the fire?"

"No."

"Do you pour water over a fire to put it out?"

"No. Of course not."

"Have you ever cut down a cedar tree or any of the evergreens?"

"Never."

"When you wake up in the morning, what do you do?"

"Why, like everyone else, I go to the water."

Gone-in-the-Water puffed some more.

"You see?" he asked.

"Well, no, I don't think so. I'm not sure."

"You know all these things. You don't need the priests to tell you what to do and what not to do. We all know. None of us need them. And as long as our children are taught to do the right things, there will never be a need for priests."

"I see," said Edohi. "But there is another thing."

"Yes?"

"The priests are Real People. They are people of the seven clans."

"And each of the seven clans, I hear, has renounced them and declared them enemies and promised there will be no clan revenge."

"But the clan revenge is to maintain the balance, is it not? If a man of my clan should kill a man of the Wolf Clan, we are out of balance until the Wolf People kill one of us."

"Yes," said Gone-in-the-Water, "but if all seven clans are there in Men's Town, then some will be killed from each clan. There will be no revenge after the fight, and everything remains in balance. There is no problem there."

The old man sucked in vain on his pipe stem.

"The tobacco is all smoked," he said. "Are you satisfied, nephew?"

"Yes, Uncle. I am satisfied. Thank you."

Edohi stood up and walked to the door. He bent over and stepped outside. Gone-in-the-Water followed him as far as the doorway.

"There's something you didn't ask me about," he said. "Most men would have asked."

Edohi turned back to face the old man.

"What's that, Uncle?" he asked.

"I've already asked and looked, and I've been told. In the fight, you will prevail."

Sixteen

STANDING-IN-THE-DOORWAY paced impatiently along the edge of the mound there in front of the temple. Two Heads had not returned. Neither had the two warrior-priests he had sent to kill Edohi. They should all three have come back before dark, and it was dark. On an ordinary night, he would have already been asleep, or at least lying in his bed. Lying in his bed with Two Heads. He did not want to go to his bed alone. He had posted sentries along the wall, and torches lined the path that led to the entryway to Men's Town. There were a couple of men posted out there, too.

"Ah, Two Heads," he said. "Two Heads, where are you?"

The other two didn't matter. Of course, he wanted Edohi dead, but others could be sent out to do that job if these two had indeed failed. He paced some more. Why did they not return? Then he heard footsteps coming up

the mound to the temple, and his heart jumped in antici-
pation. But it was not Two Heads. It was another priest,
one he had sent out to watch the road from Ijodi. The
man's name was Ashes.

"What is it?" said Standing-in-the-Doorway.

"There are some people here from Ijodi," said Ashes.
"They say that they must speak with you."

"Bring them to me," said Standing-in-the-Doorway.
"Hurry."

"There are women with them," said Ashes.

"Bring them all."

The priest rushed away, and Standing-in-the-Doorway
resumed his pacing. People from Ijodi might know something about Two Heads and about the other two. He had
an impulse to rush down to meet them, but he restrained
himself. Ashes came back with the visitors from Ijodi.
They were the ones who had remained loyal to the *Ani-
Kutani*, the ones who had been left out of the recent meetings in Ijodi and the meeting at Kanasta.

"Have you seen Two Heads?" Standing-in-the-Doorway asked immediately. As fast as he said the words, he
realized that he should not have seemed so anxious.

"He came to Ijodi," said a woman. "The people were
all gone. All but us. He asked us where they went, and we
told him toward Kanasta. He left to go there, I think."

"And he didn't return?"

"No."

"Why had the people gone to Kanasta?"

"We believe that they are planning to attack you," said
a man. "They've been holding secret meetings. They

won't tell us anything. When we approach them, they stop talking."

"They had been talking loudly against you," said the woman. "Then they stopped. All at once. And that was when the secret meetings began."

"Are these people still at Kanasta?" asked Standing-in-the-Doorway.

"They returned to Ijodi and went into their homes," said the woman.

"But they were still awake," said the man, "puttering about inside their homes. I think they're preparing their weapons."

Standing-in-the-Doorway turned to Ashes, who was still standing there awaiting further instructions.

"Tell every man to get his weapons," he said. "Get yours, too. Then come back here to me."

Ashes hurried away, and Standing-in-the-Doorway paced for a moment in front of the people from Ijodi.

"Did you come here armed?" he demanded.

"Yes," said the man. "They made us leave our weapons down below."

"Will you stay and fight with us?"

"Yes. We will."

"We all will," said the woman.

"How many of you are here?"

"We are twenty."

"Good. Go back down and get your weapons. Wait there until you hear more."

They left, and he was again alone. He wondered what had become of Two Heads. He had gone to Ijodi, and then he had followed the conspirators to Kanasta. The conspirators had returned to Ijodi, but not, apparently, Two Heads. And he had not returned to Men's Town. Standing-in-the-Doorway tried not to believe his worst fears. He had to get his mind on immediate problems. It seemed from what he had just been told that Ijodi was in revolt. Then Ijodi would have to be destroyed, Ijodi and everyone in it, everyone except those few loyal ones who had come to Men's Town. If the revolt was not put down swiftly and decisively, other towns might follow the example of Ijodi. The power and authority of Men's Town must be asserted firmly or all could be lost.

He wondered if Ijodi would attack or if it would simply arm itself and declare its independence from Men's Town. Either way, the best course of action for Men's Town, he decided, would be to attack Ijodi and take them by surprise. Ashes came back up on the mound.

"Everyone is getting armed," he said.

"Good. Go down again and gather everyone together down there below where I can speak to them. Leave the sentries on the wall. They can hear me well enough, but bring in those from out on the road. And set some torches here so that I may be seen."

The light from the flickering torches played across his face, giving him a mysterious and frightening aspect there on the mound above the crowd, making it all the easier for them to imagine him to be somehow something more than merely human. He stood there with his arms across his chest looking out into the black sky, not looking down, appearing to be unaware of or unconcerned about their presence there below him. They waited anxiously for his words, waited in silence, holding their breath until forced to expel it and draw in more night air. At last he spoke.

"My children," he said, "listen to me. Ijodi is in revolt. You may have friends there. We all have relatives among them. They are Real People, people of the seven clans. But they have forfeited their rights by this revolt. You must put aside your feelings for these people, and count them bitter enemies. Look for examples on these few here from Ijodi, loyal ones who have come to warn us and to join us in our fight.

"Consider this. These disobedient ones would bring destruction on us all. One among them refused to do his part for the ancient ceremony, thereby risking the weakening of its effectiveness. That ceremony was to bring us rain. Another has been in open mourning since the ceremony. All of them there in Ijodi, except these loyal few here with us, all of them have been speaking against us and disparaging our efforts on their behalf.

"Earlier today I sent three priests to Ijodi to investigate the rumors I had heard. They have not returned, and I fear—I fear for their safety."

He paused and turned his back to the crowd and waited. He could hear the murmurs down below.

"Look," someone said. "He's overcome with emotion."

"He's a great man," said another, "and he has great compassion."

Standing-in-the-Doorway turned back again to face them, and they again fell silent.

"Be up and armed and dressed for war before the Sun shows herself in the morning. We will march on Ijodi and put down this rebellion, and the blood in the streets of Ijodi will bring the rain."

She had watched as the people returned to Ijodi from Kanasta, but she had not seen her son again. Of course, she told herself, Two Heads might have gone back to Men's Town by another route. That was a possibility. But he was her son, and she was worried. The people, most of them, were very angry at the priests. They might do anything.

And she was alone. She could not join in with the malcontents and rail against her only son. Yet she couldn't convince herself that the killing of the Spoiler's daughter had been justified, and she could not align herself with those who did. She understood the Spoiler's rage. She even sympathized. And there was Two Heads himself. He wasn't like her son anymore. He was aloof. He had no time for his own mother. And she saw the arrogance he displayed toward others. Somewhere along the way, she knew, she had lost him. Where, she asked herself, and how? What did she do that she should not have done, or what had she failed to do? She tried, but she could not find the answers to those questions.

When the Sun was low and the sky was getting dim, she had left her house. She had tried to leave Ijodi without being seen, but she had not been successful. Anyway, she had told herself, it didn't really matter. So she had been seen. She had walked to the river, and then she had walked along its bank. She had known just where she was going. There was a spot ahead, a place she knew. She had not been there for a while, but she knew the way. As the evening turned to night, she stumbled along in the darkness. She knew where she was going, but she did not know where all the rocks, deadfall, driftwood and depressions lay in her path. She stumbled along.

She knew she was getting close when she found herself climbing. The way grew steeper with each step. At last she found herself standing on the edge of a high precipice overlooking the river. The wall below her was not straight. A rock dropped off from the top would hit the wall several times before landing on the space of rocky shore below. But it was high, and it was sure.

She stood on the edge, and she could hear the rush of the waters below. She would not reach the water, she knew. She spread her arms. She lifted her head and looked toward the stars. She leaned forward until she lost her balance and fell. For a brief, exhilarating moment, she felt as though she was flying. Then she hit. She knew that bones were broken, but there was no pain, just a powerful shock followed by an overwhelming dullness. She bounced, and when she hit the second time, she felt no more. The lifeless body bounced again and hit again and tumbled to rest at last on the rocks below.

The Spoiler laid out her weapons. She had a bow and a few arrows, a knife and a warclub. They had belonged to her husband, and she had used them before. It had been a good many years since then, but she would use them again. Standing outside her door, the Outcast watched her with interest and undisguised admiration.

"You're going to fight?" he said.

"Yes."

"I think I knew you would. May I help? May I fight, too?"

"I told you before," she said, "do what you want. You're free."

"When Edohi brought me to you, he gave you my weapons."

"Oh. That's right. They're over there."

She nodded her head toward a corner of her house, and the Outcast ducked his head to go inside and locate his weapons. He found them and gathered them together. The Spoiler had made all her preparations. Suddenly she had nothing more to do, and she was there alone in her house with the Outcast. She looked at him with wonder.

"Why are you doing this?" she said.

"For you," he said.

The Spoiler studied the Outcast for a moment. He was completely sincere in his desire to support her in any way he could. She was sure of that. And this was the same man she had insulted. She had threatened to kill him. She had called him a dog and treated him as such. So why was he behaving in this way toward her? Was she so desirable? At her age? She found that explanation hard to believe, yet there was no other. And he was a handsome man. And a good one. And brave and bold. His command of her own language was so complete that it was almost possible to forget that he was not one of the Real People, that he was a Shawnee, a hated enemy.

"Outcast," she said.

"Yes?"

"When the fight is over, when we have won, if you and

I have both survived, I will take you for my husband, if that is what you want."

She amazed herself that she had said it, but it was done, and she waited defensively for his response.

"That is the only thing I want," he said. "You've just made me very happy. We will survive, you and I."

"Then in the meantime," said the Spoiler, "we have some time to wait before we go to Men's Town. There is a chance that one or both of us will die tomorrow, in spite of what you say. Spend that time here with me."

She pulled her deerskin dress off over her head and dropped it to the floor, and she stood there radiant in her nakedness, inviting the Outcast to come to her. She didn't have to wait for long.

Seventeen

STANDING-IN-THE-DOORWAY had not slept. He knew that the night would soon be over. The Sun would make her appearance in the east crawling back under the edge of the Sky Vault. He could hear down below some of the people already beginning to stir. He pulled on his white doeskin leggings and fastened them to a band around his waist. Then he pulled his breechclout between his legs and secured it at the waist, front and back. He put on his moccasins, stretched himself to his full height and walked around his little room, loosening his muscles. He slipped a fresh, beige-colored, woven robe over his head. It reached almost to his knees. Then he wrapped a woven sash twice around his waist and tied it, leaving the long, tasseled ends dangling a little below the bottom of the robe. The sash had been made of strands of material dyed red and yellow, put together in such a way as to present a red background with a jagged streak of lightning running its full length.

He hung around his neck, covering himself from the clavicle to just above the waist, a breastplate made of a series of slightly overlapping horizontal slats of hardwood bound together with rawhide thongs. And over all he draped his dark, turkey feather cape, which hung behind him all the way to his heels. His headdress he put on last. A skullcap of netting, it fit his head snugly and was decorated around its banded edge with black and white beads. White crane feathers tufted with red stood up straight from the band all the way around his head, taller in front than in the back.

He dipped his two forefingers into a small pot on a shelf on the wall and smeared a horizontal vermilion streak under each eye. Finally he took up in his left hand his disc-shaped buffalo hide shield, and in his right his war axe. An upright hand, an eyeball in its palm, was painted in the center of the shield, and circling the hand were two rattlesnakes, each biting the other on the tail just behind the rattles. The axe was finely fashioned from one piece of stone and polished smooth. It was heavy, but his right arm was strong. Thus prepared, he stepped out of his room to stand on the upper ledge of the mound. He was pleased to see that his warriors were already prepared and were gathered there below, waiting.

Anywhere other than in the immediate overwhelming presence of Standing-in-the-Doorway, Ashes was an imposing figure. An old warrior, he had risen as far as he could in the ranks of the *Ani-Kutani*, and he was secretly resentful of Two Heads, who, when not much more than a child, had been placed immediately at the right hand of Standing-in-the-Doorway. Ashes knew the reason for the meteoric rise of Two Heads. Most of the priests knew. But they all assumed that the great man had both a right to and a reason for his strange proclivities. Still, Ashes thought, it should be possible for Standing-in-the-Doorway to keep a young man for his pleasure without giving him rank and power. But Ashes was an old soldier, and he did his job.

On this particular morning, his job was to lead the army out of Men's Town to the attack on Ijodi. He was dressed and armed similarly to Standing-in-the-Doorway, but, of course, his dress was a little less resplendent. On orders from Standing-in-the-Doorway, a few men were left in the town, armed and on watch on the walls. Ashes sent out four scouts, allowed them to get well ahead, then walked out of Men's Town alone. His army followed him, and when the last warrior had passed through the narrow passageway to leave the town, four priests brought up the rear, carrying on their shoulders the chair in which Standing-in-the-Doorway sat, haughty, aloof and alert.

It was about midway between Men's Town and Ijodi. The Sun was barely peeking over the eastern horizon, beginning to light the sky. Stinging Ant had gone ahead of the others from Ijodi, and he was up near the ridge of the mountain overlooking the road. He saw down below two priests on the road. They were armed, and they were looking around cautiously. Stinging Ant was about to turn to run back and report to Edohi what he had seen, but another movement below caught his eye. There was a third *Kutani*. He was off the road on the river side. Three scouts? Had Men's Town discovered the Ijodi plot and sent its own army out to meet them? Or were they planning to attack Ijodi? If these three were scouts, would there be a fourth? He studied the mountainside below, and soon he found the man. There were four, two on the road, and one off on each side. The main body of warriors would not be far behind.

Stinging Ant, taking care to keep himself concealed from the scouts, hurried back to Edohi. He found him at the head of his army. Edohi had told them to meet him at Men's Town, but when he had been ready to leave in the early morning, they had been there, and they had been ready to go. There were at least two hundred of them, and they all left together, all except Stinging Ant, who had gone ahead to scout.

"Edohi," he said, "there are four priests coming this way. They're armed for battle. Two are on the road, and two are off, one on each side. I think they're scouts."

"If they're scouts," said Edohi, "that means that the *Ani-Kutani* are coming in force. They might be planning to attack Ijodi, or, if they somehow found out about our plans, they would be coming to meet us. Pass the word along to everyone. Tell them to spread out and hide themselves. We'll let these four walk into our trap."

The warriors did as Edohi said, and soon they were all hidden. No one was on the road. No one was visible anywhere. Then they waited. They waited but not for long. The priest on the river side of the road was the first to reach the line of concealed warriors. He walked past Beavertail, who was hidden there in the brush. Beavertail let the priest continue on a few paces, then he stood, nocked an arrow and let it fly. It struck the unsuspecting scout between the shoulder blades. The man stiffened, then fell forward dead. On the opposite side of the road, Hemp Carrier came out of hiding to grab a *Kutani* scout around the throat from behind. Stinging Ant appeared and stabbed the man in the heart. Just then half a dozen warriors rushed out onto the road to swarm around the two remaining scouts, swinging their warclubs. In short order, the two lay dead in the road in pools of their own blood, bludgeoned to death.

It was daylight. Edohi had the four bodies laid out together on the road, and then he called for the other three, the two he and Hemp Carrier had killed on the mountain and that of Two Heads. Seven dead priests lay in the road. It would be too much trouble to lug the seven bodies along, yet he wanted them when they reached the walls of Men's Town, or, he reminded himself, when they encountered the Men's Town army along the road.

"Uncle," he said.

"Yes?" said Hemp Carrier.

"Have the heads cut off these seven to carry along with us."

A big man standing nearby had overheard. He stepped forward somewhat anxiously, wielding a large stone axe.

"Let me do it," he said. "My axe is sharp."

Edohi gave the man an affirmative nod, and the man went cheerfully to work. Edohi looked around.

"Stinging Ant," he said.

"I'm here," said Stinging Ant.

"Go out again and see how far behind their army is."

Stinging Ant started back up the mountainside at a run. Soon he was out of sight. The big man with the sharp stone axe was already at work on the third body.

"What now, Edohi?" said Hemp Carrier.

"As soon as he's done here," said Edohi, "we'll take up those heads and go on toward Men's Town."

Edohi walked in the center of the road ahead of everyone else. The seven men nearest him each carried a *Kutani* head, clutching it by the long, loose scalplock, letting it dangle by his side as he walked. Stinging Ant came down the mountainside at a run. He stopped in front of Edohi and pointed ahead on the road.

"They are just around that bend in the road," he said. "It looks like almost every priest from Men's Town is there. Even Standing-in-the-Doorway is with them. He's in his chair at the rear."

Edohi looked to both sides of the road. He looked at the bend in the road ahead and then back at the people gathered there behind him.

"This is as good a place as any," he said. Then he turned to the seven men carrying the heads. "Place them here in their path," he said. The first was placed in the center of the road, one on each side of it near the two edges. Then the next three were set four paces behind those. One was left. It was that of Two Heads, and it was held by the man who had severed them all. Already he was being called by a new name, Cuts-Off-Their-Heads. "Keep that one for now," said Edohi, and he turned again to face the crowd behind him.

"We thought we were going to Men's Town," he said,

"but they have come out to meet us. Once again, spread out and hide yourselves. Stay out of sight until they get right here and recognize their friends. Then shoot your arrows. Kill as many as you can from hiding with your arrows."

He watched them as they hid themselves. From out in the road, he could not see them. Good, he thought, neither will the *Ani-Kutani*. Now to hide himself. But first he went to the spot where he had seen Cuts-Off-Their-Heads duck down behind some large rocks at the side of the road.

"Cuts-Off-Their-Heads," he said.

The man seemed to beam with pride at the sound of his new name.

"Yes, Edohi?"

"I want that one. May I have it?"

Cuts-Off-Their-Heads held the grisly object out toward Edohi for him to take.

"He might have another one somewhere," he said.

"What?" said Edohi.

"Wasn't this the one called Two Heads?"

"Oh, yes," said Edohi. "I think his other one was between his legs."

He took the head and hurried to a spot up on the mountainside behind a large, smooth boulder. His view of the road was good from there. He put the head down on the ground by his left side, and he laid out all his arrows within easy reach. He felt amazingly alive. He thought that he could almost feel the blood racing through his veins. He was anxious for the coming battle as he had not been anxious for anything for some time. He was excited.

But he was the leader, and he was responsible for the lives of all those who followed him. He remembered the Outcast and how he had gotten his name. He had to think of all the others. He hoped, therefore, that they would be able to strike a decisive blow with their arrows. If the arrows ran out before the priests were all killed, or if the priests should manage somehow to get through the arrows, the combat would be hand-to-hand, axe-to-axe, warclub-to-warclub and knife-to-knife. Then it would be bloody on both sides. Edohi hoped that they would not see very much of that kind of fighting.

Eighteen

ASHES WASN'T WORRIED about the bend in the road ahead. He had four scouts out to warn him of any danger that might be waiting there. He fully expected to march directly to Ijodi and then to lead an attack. If anyone had been coming from Ijodi, he thought, surely the scouts would have already reported back to him. He rounded the bend, and he saw something strange in the road ahead. They were no more than dark spots, and they could have been six large rocks. The strangeness was in the pattern. There were two even rows of three each. It was not a natural pattern. He walked on ahead, his army following, and then he saw what they were. He stopped, astonished, and he held up his hand for a general halt. He walked on then, slowly and alone, and he recognized the faces of his four scouts, and he recognized the faces of the two men who had been sent to kill Edohi and had not returned.

"What is it?" shouted Standing-in-the-Doorway from his chair behind the army.

Just then Ashes realized what he had done. He knew that he had led his army into a trap. He knew it, but as soon as he knew it, the people began to appear. They appeared from behind trees, from depressions in the ground, from down in the tall, dry grass, from behind bushes and bramble and boulders. They appeared on both sides of the road, on the slope toward the river to his left, and on the mountainside to his right. And as they appeared, they shot their arrows. Ashes had very little time in which to reflect on his mistake. He fell there in front of the ghastly, staring heads with three arrows in his chest.

A shower of arrows rained down on the front ranks of the *Ani-Kutani*, and the narrow road was soon paved with their bodies. Their comrades to the rear were stepping on them in their attempt to get to the front to fight back. The army of priests had been thrown into confusion by the sudden fierce attack and by the loss of their leader. The four priests carrying Standing-in-the-Doorway even moved up closer as the army from Men's Town pressed forward. From his place behind the boulder on the mountainside, Edohi saw that Standing-in-the-Doorway was just down there beneath him. He was very near.

Edohi grabbed the hair of the head there beside him, and he swung the head around in a circle four times, then let it go. It flew in a high arc and came down in the lap of Standing-in-the-Doorway. Standing-in-the-Doorway screamed in surprised horror and recoiled. He jerked apart his knees, and the head fell between his feet, rolling over to stare up at him, and he saw the face. Just then an arrow struck his right, front bearer, and that corner of the chair dropped as the man fell. The pole broke, and Standing-in-the-Doorway and the bloody head together went tumbling to the ground.

"Fall back. Fall back," he shouted, and he scrambled to his feet and turned and ran.

The three remaining bearers were the first to follow him. Then others still at the rear saw what had happened, and they too turned to run. A half-dozen bold *Ani-Kutani* warriors near the front decided to counterattack, and they ran over and beyond the bodies of their fallen comrades, brandishing warclubs and axes and gobbling like turkeys. All six were brought down in the road with arrows before any of them got close to any of their attackers. Then there was no one left but the dead and dying. Standing-in-the-Doorway and those who had joined him in flight were gone. Edohi and his army emerged from their places of concealment and went back down to the road. They inspected the carnage there, and when they found a wounded priest, yet alive, they crushed his skull or cut his throat or plunged a knife into his heart. When they were done, there was not a man or woman among them whose hands were not bloody, and not a one was hurt.

Edohi estimated that they had killed half of the army from Men's Town. There was shouting and rejoicing, and Edohi had a difficult time getting their attention, getting them to stop dancing in the gore, to stop shouting and laughing, to listen to him once again.

"It's not over," he said at last. "We've done well here, but there's more yet to do. The rest have run away. They're probably going back into Men's Town, and we will have to attack them behind their wall after all. Come on. Let's go."

He turned and ran after the fleeing priests. They were already well ahead and out of sight, but there was no place for them to go but Men's Town. When he reached the bend in the road, he looked back over his shoulder. It looked like everyone was coming. He slowed his pace to allow them to catch up with him. When Hemp Carrier came up beside him, he caught his uncle by the arm to slow him. They let the others pass them by, and they walked along behind.

"Let them go," Edohi said. "They'll slow down soon, I think. Or if they run all the way to Men's Town, that's all right too."

"If the priests get inside the walls before we catch them," said Hemp Carrier, "what will we do?"

"I don't know yet," said Edohi. "Let's just get them trapped in there, and then we'll see."

Gone-in-the-Water came walking along the road. He moved slowly, with a walking stick in his right hand. He had followed the army as it left Ijodi that morning, but it had quickly outdistanced him.

"Ah, you've come back, have you?" he said, looking down toward the road in front of him. "You thought that just because all the others ran off from me, you two would do the same. Just because I'm an old man, you do me that way. One of these days, you'll be old, too. Both of you. Then you'll find out what it's like. Then you'll wish that you'd shown more respect to your elders. You— You what? Found what? Dead men? Just up the road? Well, come on then. Let's go."

He hurried on as fast as he could make himself go. At last he came to the site of the recent ambush. He saw the bodies, and he saw the six heads there in the road.

"Ah," he said, "they did all right, didn't they? These are all priests. Every one. We told them Edohi was the one, didn't we? Yes. He's done all right here today."

He walked through the carnage, looking at the faces, recognizing some of them, calling some by name. He picked his way through to the rear of the battle site, and there he saw the wreckage of the abandoned litter chair.

"Ha," he said. "Look at that. So the great man was spilled onto the dirt. I wish I had seen that."

He cackled at the image that formed in his mind, but then he saw the seventh severed head close by, and he squatted down there by it and studied the face in silence for a moment.

"Not so proud now, young man, are you?" he said. "No. Now he's not so proud."

He stood up again and studied the chair for a while, and then he came to a decision.

"Come on, Ugly," he said. "Noisy. Help me here. Gather up all the dead wood you can find and pile it on this chair. A big pile for a big fire."

By the time he decided that the pile was big enough, he was tired from all the work. He had to sit down and rest and catch his breath. But he was proud of the pile of wood that nearly covered the chair. When he finally began to breathe evenly again, he reached into the pouch which hung at his side and drew out his fire-making sticks. Then he stood up and walked over to the wood pile which covered Standing-in-the-Doorway's chair. He got down on his knees and went to work, and soon he had a fire. When he saw that the fire was going to grow, he labored back up to his feet. He got the head of Two Heads by its hair and carelessly tossed it in. Then he started walking back toward the bodies and the other heads.

"Come on, you two," he said. "We have a lot of work to do here today."

They were almost to Men's Town when the Spoiler left the crowd to go her own way. The Outcast wondered what she was up to, but he didn't question her. He just followed along. If she wanted him to know, she would tell him. The Spoiler's brother, Agili, also noticed, and he, too, followed. He didn't wonder, though, for long where his sister was going. They had walked for only a little way when he knew where she was going, and he knew why. Up ahead was a house, and beside the house stood an arbor. A cooking fire burned in front of the house, but no one was in sight. The Spoiler stopped in front of the house about six paces away. She stood with her hands on her hips as her two male companions stopped beside her, one on each side. Then she called out.

"War Woman. Are you in there?"

War Woman stepped out of the house. She looked at her three visitors. They were stern, menacing.

"What do you want here?" she said.

The Spoiler didn't answer her. Instead, she spoke to the men there with her.

"Why did you two follow me here," she said, "to watch or to help?"

"We came to help," said the Outcast.

"What do you want, sister?" said Agili.

"Take her and tie her," said the Spoiler.

The men moved toward War Woman, and she dodged back into her house. Just as they reached her door, she reappeared, a warclub in her hand. Agili grabbed her wrist and twisted. The Outcast held her other arm. She struggled against them, but Agili's strength overcame hers, and she dropped the warclub. They dragged her to the arbor and tied her wrists to the two upright end poles on the end nearest the house. Then, at the Spoiler's insistence, they also tied her ankles to the poles. She was spread-eagled standing upright. The Spoiler stepped up to her, knife in hand. She stared hard into War Woman's eyes, and then she cut and tore away the deerskin dress that covered War Woman's body.

"So she was in Men's Town," the Spoiler said. "So I can relax. So everything will be all right. You talked to your brother, did you?"

Suddenly she drove the knife into War Woman's naked flesh, deep and low in the belly. War Woman clenched her teeth and ground them together. Her face twisted with the pain, but she made no sound. Then the Spoiler ripped upward with the knife, and War Woman's body hung limp. The Spoiler turned away, her front covered with the other's blood.

"Burn this whole place down," she said.

Nineteen

W HEN THE ARMY from Ijodi had run almost half the distance from the site of their ambush to Men's Town, they began to slow down. They were tiring, and they figured that the priests were already inside the wall anyway. They walked the rest of the way. A *Kutani* on the wall shouted an alarm when he saw them, and Beavertail shot him through the chest with an arrow. The man dropped out of sight behind the wall. For a short while after that, no one appeared on the wall. Then four men showed themselves up there, but just barely. They didn't stand up tall the way the sentries at Men's Town usually did. They crouched low and peered out over the edge. Outside, the army from Ijodi milled about. Some shouted threats, taunts and insults at the walls. Occasionally someone tried a bowshot at one of the sentries, but the shots went wild. The sentries were staying down.

"Let's go in there and get them," said Beavertail.

"I think we should wait for Edohi," said Stinging Ant. "He might have a plan."

"What plan can he have?" Beavertail argued. "The priests are in there, and we're out here. Edohi said we should kill them all. That's his plan. We can't kill them from out here, so let's go in after them."

"It's too dangerous," said Stinging Ant. "The passageway is too narrow."

"They won't even fight us," said Beavertail. "They ran from us already. I'm going in. Who's going with me?"

He raised his warclub over his head and gave a loud, piercing gobble. Without looking back, he ran toward the entry to the passageway, a narrow lane formed by the parallel overlapping of the two ends of the wall which surrounded the town. A woman and four men made the sound of the turkey, waved their weapons, and followed him. Cuts-Off-Their-Heads stepped over to stand beside Stinging Ant.

"You were right," he said. "They'll all be killed."

"There's nothing we can do," said Stinging Ant.

Beavertail reached the entry and turned sharply to run through the long, narrow lane between the walls. He could hear the gobbling close behind him, so he knew that others were following. He could see the end of the lane up ahead, and he saw no priests there. His way into the town was open. But when he burst through into the open, an arrow sank into his chest. He staggered to a halt and fell forward, landing on the arrow, driving it the rest of the way through his body. The next warrior came through the passageway into the town and saw the body of Beavertail just ahead just as two priests came from around the corner of the wall swinging their clubs.

Outside, Stinging Ant and the others couldn't see what was happening. They could hear the turkey sounds, shouts and shrieks. They watched the wall and waited. Edohi and Hemp Carrier arrived, and Edohi found Stinging Ant.

"What's happening in there?" he asked.

Stinging Ant told him about the brief argument he had had with Beavertail.

"But he wouldn't listen," he said. "He went in anyway, and five others went with him."

The shouting stopped, and the silence which followed was deathly still. The evening air was hot and dusty. It had been a long day, and Edohi was tired. Now he was angry at Beavertail. They had killed half the priests without so much as a hurt on their side. Now Beavertail's foolishness would take care of that. There would be six dead. Then they saw movement on the wall. Two priests appeared. They tossed a body over the wall, then another, and then a third.

"They've killed them all," said Cuts-Off-Their-Heads.

"Uncle," said Edohi, "when they show themselves again, shoot for the one on your right."

Edohi nocked an arrow, and so did Hemp Carrier. They waited. Then the two priests appeared again and heaved a fourth body over the wall. Just as they released the body, Edohi and Hemp Carrier released their arrows. Both hit their marks. Both priests slumped behind the wall.

"What now, Edohi?" said Hemp Carrier.

"Soon it will be dark," said Edohi. "We'll spread ourselves out all the way around Men's Town. Some of us will sleep, and some will watch. If a *Kutani* shows himself, or if one comes out of town, we'll kill him. Otherwise we'll do nothing. Not until morning."

"I'll tell everyone and see that it's done," said Hemp Carrier.

Standing-in-the-Doorway did not go up to his private room. The mound was so high that someone outside the walls could shoot at anyone who dared show himself up there, and he did not want to give them that chance with his body. Not just yet. So he stayed down below with everyone else. They could not come into town, he told himself. That had already been demonstrated. A few men could hold off an army at the end of the narrow passage, for men could enter through it only in single file. The only other way into town was over the walls, and that, too, was impractical. The wall was high, too high for a man to jump and catch the edge. They would have to climb on each other's shoulders or on a climbing pole, and that would take time. Men on the wall could easily pick them off while they were trying it. And fire? The walls were plastered smooth with mud and would not burn. No. They could not get in. The only danger was in exposing one's self on the wall or on top of the mound. The only immediate danger.

The real danger, he knew, was not immediate. It was a long-range danger. Eventually they would run out of food and water there inside the wall. How long would that

take? Would the wretched army of rebels hold itself together for a long enough siege to win the battle by starva-
tion? And what about the other towns? As time wore on,
would they join in the siege or would they decide that the
rebels were wrong and come to the aid of the priests?
These were things he could not know, but they were the
things, he thought, that would determine his fate. And not
just his alone. The fate of Men's Town, the fate of the
Real People, the fate of the world was at stake. Did those
fools out there not know? Had they forgotten? Or was
this the way the world was supposed to end?

It was dark, and the air was still hot and dry. Dust
seemed to hover over all like a low-lying cloud. The entire population of a town of the Real People was in actual
and open revolt against their ancient priesthood, the *Ani-
Kutani*, an action beyond belief, unthinkable until it had
occurred. And Two Heads was gone. The horrible image
of the severed head seemed to loom before him. He
couldn't drive it away. No matter what other thoughts,
what fears, he had with which to occupy his mind, the
haunting, ghastly image hovered still.

Edohi did not sleep that night. He circled Men's Town
several times, talking to the people he found awake, making sure that they were there, that they were watching. He
watched the wall himself as he walked around the town,
and he thought about ways of getting through to the *Ani-
Kutani*. When at last he knew that the Sun would soon be
showing herself to begin a new day, he went to find some
of the Wolf People. Big Foot, Trotting Wolf and Cuts-
Off-Their-Heads were there.

"Have you brought fire as I asked?" said Edohi.

"I have my fire-starting sticks," said Big Foot.

"I've brought some hot coals in a pot," said Trotting Wolf.

"Good," said Edohi. "Go with them to the wall before the Sun appears. Set fire to the wall."

"The mud won't burn," said Big Foot.

"The wood inside is old and dry," said Edohi. "If you break through the mud, the wood will burn."

"I'll go with my axe," said Cuts-Off-Their-Heads. "I'll chop through and expose the wood."

"Get some others to help," Edohi said. "Light it in four places around the town. And take someone else along. Someone with a bow and arrows to watch the wall above."

Edohi wasn't sure that the fire would work inside the hardened mud, but it was worth a try, he thought, and he had called for four different fires. One of them might work. He knew that fire needed air, but the walls were old, and here and there were cracks. It might just work. From where he waited he could see Trotting Wolf and Cuts-Off-Their-Heads. The others had gone to other parts of the wall. So far no one had appeared on the wall above where the two men were working. He could see that Cuts-Off-Their-Heads had stepped back from the wall, and Trotting Wolf was down on his knees close to it. In a short while, Trotting Wolf stood up, backed away, then turned and ran with Cuts-Off-Their-Heads back toward Edohi. By then Edohi could see the red glow at the base of the wall, and then he felt a breeze.

By the time the Sun had lit the sky, smoke was pouring from several cracks in the wall, and the breeze had become a strong wind out of the west. Suddenly from one of the cracks in the wall which had been spewing smoke, flames burst forth. Some wanted to rush the town right then, but Edohi held them back.

"Let it burn," he said. "After a while, it will crumble. Then we'll rush through where it falls."

They waited and watched as the fire increased, and from where he stood, Edohi could see that at least one of the other three fires was growing on the opposite side of the town. He had his instructions relayed around the perimeter: when a piece of the wall falls, attack.

And then it happened, and then they ran for the breach in the wall, Edohi leading the assault. Four warriors side by side and four behind them and then four more and more and more rushed through the flames and the smoke invading Men's Town. They were met immediately by a defensive line of *Ani-Kutani*. Edohi cracked one's skull with his warclub, and on either side of him a warrior chopped down a priest. On the far side of the town, another section of wall collapsed. Another wave of invaders rushed into the town.

Fanned by the wind, flames ate away at the Men's Town wall in several different places, and the town itself was filled with fierce combatants. But the invaders outnumbered the priests, and everyone could tell that the outcome was inevitable. Warrior-priests desired only to take one or two with them before they themselves were killed.

Near the breach through which he had entered the town, Hemp Carrier faced a *Kutani*. Both men were armed with warclubs. Hemp Carrier swung his club at the priest's head, but the *Kutani* was quick. With his own club, he blocked the blow, and Hemp Carrier lost his weapon. With his left hand, he drew his knife from the sheath at his waist and plunged it into the breast of the priest. Before the body hit the ground, Hemp Carrier was looking around for his next victim. The Spoiler and the Outcast, having rejoined the others sometime in the night, fought side by side. But it was becoming difficult to find opponents. Three and four attackers found themselves with only one priest to assault.

At the base of the steps which led up the mound to the front of the temple, Standing-in-the-Doorway chopped down an invader with his great stone axe. Then he turned and ran up the steps. Two more of the assaulting warriors followed him, one carrying a flaming faggot from the wall. As they reached the top of the mound, Standing-in-the-Doorway swung his axe again. It crashed into the side of the head of one, and as the body pitched headlong off the mound, the other man tossed his torch into the temple. Standing-in-the-Doorway turned and buried the blade of his axe between the man's shoulder blades. But he had turned his back to the steps, and another man came running up. He flung himself at the priest, warclub high, just as Standing-in-the-Doorway turned back around. The *Kutani* blocked the blow, but the force of the man crashing into him carried them both through the doorway into the temple. They staggered across the room struggling with each other, and they knocked into the altar there in the middle of the room, the altar on which the sacred fire burned. Standing-in-the-Doorway's cloak burst into flame as the altar overturned. He shrieked and swung his axe, splitting his opponent's skull. Then he ran back out the door.

He stood at the top of the stairs aflame.

"It's the end of the world," he shouted, and an arrow shot from below struck him in the chest. He staggered back and fell, his burning body half in, half out of the temple on the mound.

Twenty

THERE WERE a few priests yet fighting, but they were all dispatched in short order. Then it was all over. It was over except for the celebrating, the boasting, the mutual congratulations, the dispassionate execution of any *Kutani* discovered yet alive. No one had escaped the wrath of the army from Ijodi. And they deliberately spread the fire. They touched flames to all the buildings in the town. The temple was already burning but not fast enough to suit them. Some ran into various rooms in the temple to spread the fire, and in the process smashed the pots and the pieces of sculpture they found there. In one room, Cuts-Off-Their-Heads found rows and rows of folded, pounded bark "leaves" which were covered with strange little marks. He lit them with his torch.

Edohi felt suddenly strange. The sense of elation was still with him, but there was nothing more to be done. There was no one left to fight, no more priests to kill. It was all over, abruptly, at once. It was almost a disappointment. Then came the nausea. It came on him slowly but surely. It came from the odor of the burning town combined with the stench of death and the sight of the massacre around him. And he felt responsible, personally, for it all, and, in spite of his reassuring visit with Gone-in-the-Water, the old fear for the future returned as the sense of the enormity of what he had done came fully and clearly to his mind.

And then some began to call his name, and they called out his praises and began to gather around him. Someone cried out that Edohi should become the supreme leader of all the Real People.

"No," Edohi shouted, and he ran halfway up the steps of the mound to face them. The blood-spattered crowd below fell silent and waited for him to speak further.

"There will be no supreme leader," Edohi said. "What we have just done here—to our own people—is a thing of horror, and it was done because one man had too much power and too much authority. One man, one town made decisions for our entire nation and issued arbitrary commands to all of our people. And because of that, we slaughtered them. Nothing like that must ever happen again. There cannot be one worldly power over all of the Real People."

He knew that he was close to home, and he was anxious and in a hurry. He had taken a short cut over the mountain, and when he arrived at the ridge, he saw the fires below. It was Men's Town. There could be no mistake about that. He started down the mountain at a run, and he fell, tumbling down the mountainside. He managed to catch himself and get back to his feet. He was bruised and scratched, but nothing was broken. He was also closer to the town, and he could see that there was more below than just a fire. He saw the bodies strewn about the town, and he saw the people dancing around in celebration. His frantic mind began to sort out what must have happened there. Some enemy had attacked the town.

He ran down even closer and positioned himself behind a boulder for a better look, and then he recognized the people who were celebrating the victory. They were Real People. He should have had the sense right then to turn and run. But where would he go? For so long a time he had struggled to get back home to safety. He had been to the outside world, and he had found it to be fraught with danger. Still he should have known that only death awaited him in what was left of Men's Town. Yet he walked ahead, drawn to the flames and the carnage, drawn toward death and disaster, drawn to the horror there that he would never before have believed could ever occur.

At first, as he stumbled across the rubble in the breach where the wall had been, no one seemed to notice him. There was so much celebration going on in the town, and he was not, after all, dressed as a *Kutani*. He had been gone, too, for quite some time, and perhaps, it occurred to him, they even thought him dead somewhere in the West. He walked into the town, stepping carefully around the bodies of the butchered priests, looking at the contorted faces, and he knew them all. He was stunned and in a daze. And then he was recognized.

"Look," Stinging Ant shouted. "It's Like-a-Pumpkin returned from the West."

"Kill him," someone shouted. "He's one of them."

He saw them coming at him, and he knew that his life was about to end, not at the hands of the fierce people or of strangers in a strange land to the west, but at the hands of his own people, his friends and his relatives, the Real People, right there in his own home. He stood there. He closed his eyes, and he waited for the death blow to come.

"Stop," Edohi called. It was enough to make them hesitate at least, and he ran to stand between them and their intended final victim.

"He's a *Kutani*," said one.

"You yourself said we should kill them all," said another.

"There's been killing enough," said Edohi. "It's all over now." He thought about the small boy keeping his silent, lonely vigil outside of Kituwah. "Let him go home," he said.

Then from the west, from the source of the wind that still fanned the flames, from behind the back of Like-a-Pumpkin, came a long, low rumbling sound followed by a resounding clap of thunder that seemed to shake the ground. The people all looked toward the west, and there the sky was dark, and the rolling clouds were moving fast and coming toward them. Off to one side of the crowd, Gone-in-the-Water squatted in the dirt. He smiled, glancing down and to his right.

"You see?" he said. "He's brought the rain."

Glossary

Cherokee words, phrases and names from *The Dark Way*

Agili   He-Is-Rising, a masculine name.

Allegewi   (not Cherokee) Shawnee and Delaware name for the Cherokees. Meaning may be "Cave Dwellers." Contemporary form, Allegheny.

Ani-Gatagewi   Wild Potato People, one of the seven Cherokee clans.

Ani-Gilohi   Long Hair People, one of the seven clans.

Ani-Kawi   Deer People, one of the seven clans. (*Ani*, a plural prefix + *awi*, deer. The "k" is included to avoid a hiatus.)

Ani-Kutani   the ancient priesthood; the meaning of the word has been lost. This is the plural form.

Ani-Sakonige   Blue People, one of the seven clans.

Anisgayayi   Men's Town (*Ani* + *asgaya*, men + *yi*, "place of" or "place for.")

Ani-Tsisqua   Bird People, one of the seven clans.

Ani-Waya   Wolf People, one of the seven clans.

Ani-Wodi   Paint People, one of the seven clans.

Cheowee   an ancient town name, meaning lost.

'Chuj'   common contraction for *achuja*, boy.

Dagasi   terrapin.

Edohi He-Is-Going-About, or He-Is-Walking, a masculine name.

Gah-no-hey-nuh a traditional drink made from hominy, traditionally offered to guests.

Gatayusti a gambling game of ancient origin played with a stone disc and a throwing arrow or spear.

Ha nia li li vocables, comparable to "tra la la" in modern English song lyrics.

Hlesdi stop, quit it.

Igosdi agisdi wild lettuce.

Ijodi an ancient town name, meaning lost. Modern spelling is *Echota*.

Iya-Iyusdi *iya* (pumpkin) + *iyusdi* (like). Like-a-Pumpkin, a masculine name.

Jisdu rabbit.

Jola tobacco.

Kanasta an ancient town name, meaning lost.

Kanona a beater, a section of log or tree trunk with the top end scooped out to form a bowl shape, used with a long pole as a beater pole, like a large mortar and pestle.

Kanutche a traditional food made of pounded hickory nuts and other ingredients and served as a broth.

Kituwah an ancient town name, meaning lost. Also spelled Keetoowah. The original town was thought of as the Mother Town. Hence, Cherokees sometimes refer to themselves as Keetoowah People.

Kutani a priest (see *Ani-Kutani* above).

Mi mi mi onomatopoeic rendering of the sound made by an exhausted rabbit.

Natli ancient town name, meaning lost.

Nikutsegi   ancient town name, meaning lost. Later forms of the word are Nickajack and Nigger Jack.

Nunnehi   Immortals, mythical race of Cherokee spirit people. They are invisible and live in invisible towns. On occasion, in Cherokee lore, they have made themselves visible to come to the aid of Cherokees in a crisis. In their invisible villages, time is distorted to a mortal being.

Selu   corn, also the spirit woman who gave corn to the Cherokees.

'Siyo   contraction for *osiyo*, a greeting.

Sohi   hickory nut; also, a feminine name.

Tanasi   the name of a river, meaning lost. Contemporary form is Tennessee.

Tellico   ancient town name, meaning lost, or at least controversial. The form Tellico is still in use as a place-name in the southeast. In Oklahoma the contemporary form is Tahlequah.

Tlanuwa   a mythical giant hawk.

Tunai   a masculine name, meaning lost.

Ujonati   rattlesnake.

Ukitena   a mythical monster with a body like a giant snake, and with horns on its head and wings.

Uk'ten'   common contraction of *Ukitena*.

Wado   thank you.

Robert J. Conley is a Western writer and editor who specializes in Cherokee lore. He is the author of five previous Double D Westerns, *The Way of the Priests, Nickajack, The Saga of Henry Starr, Back to Malachi,* and *The Actor,* and received a Spur Award from the Western Writers of America for his 1987 short story "Yellow Bird." He lives in Tahlequah, Oklahoma.

Painter/pipemaker Murv Jacob, a descendant of the Kentucky Cherokees, lives and works in Tahlequah, Oklahoma. His meticulously researched, brightly colored, intricate work centers on the traditional Southeastern Indian cultures and has won numerous awards.